Ivor J. Beamon was born in Edgware, Middlesex, being one of four children, and raised in Royston, Hertfordshire. After graduating from the University of North-East London, Ivor spent the majority of his working career as a Chartered Surveyor involved in providing new homes in the UK. He always had an interest in writing as to the characters he observed and how social interactions in specific situations provide moments of humorous anecdotes that may raise a smile for others. Now the right moment had been reached to turn his back from full-time employment and put pen to paper.

I thank, Dr Gray, for his metaphoric planetary comparison of the genders in our different approach to communication and my family and friends for providing the material; even if they were unaware their situation was an inspiration to any part of my fictional ramblings.

Oh, and of course, to my wife, who captured the essence of the narrative with her cover illustration.

Ivor J. Beamon

Please Understand Me

Let's Have and
Bring up a Baby

AUSTIN MACAULEY PUBLISHERS®

LONDON • CAMBRIDGE • NEW YORK • SHARJAH

A CIP catalogue record for this title is available from the British Library.

ISBN 9781035868599 (Paperback)
ISBN 9781035868605 (ePub e-book)

www.austinmacauley.com

First Published 2024
Austin Macauley Publishers Ltd®
1 Canada Square
Canary Wharf
London
E14 5AA

Table of Contents

Foreword

The differences in how mums and dads view the skills of bringing up a baby are inextricably at odds. In the context of my observations, it triggered a curiosity as to why there is such misunderstanding of opinions and yet both genders have the same goal.

In some situations, procreation was a matter of just wham bam and out popped the children. The care for the newborn baby was just a matter of following the advice given by the professional health teams. There was no agenda to find out the whys and the wherefores of what was needed but happy in the knowledge of being passengers on a train to station, baby. In a small number of parenting couples, there is the 'alpha mum'. For these women, the desire to find out more to the nth degree, with no compromise or without taking prisoners, can lead to a greater strain on parenthood.

The different approaches and dynamics that are therefore exhibited through either the eyes of heterosexual couples or same-sex is a topic that is worthy of further exploration. There is almost always a deep sense of joy on hearing the news that in nine months, you are both to become a new parent with the first baby and the formation of a family. Of course, when a particular person believes their ascension has to attain the badge of becoming the world's greatest mum, anything less would be viewed as an abject failure. Yes, purposefully pointing out that this precondition is really about the perception of peers due to a reasonable splattering of narcissism with the alpha personality.

My contention is that it's actually okay to suggest the genders do and will have a different approach to a new life in a family environment. The nurturing goals will almost certainly be aligned in ensuring the care and welfare of a new life. Before getting too deep into the potential hapless situations of the genders, I ask the question as to how can this be when we are created with the same building blocks of DNA.

The information provided in any biology lesson was that the human egg referenced by an 'X' chromosome is impregnated by one of the millions of male sperm being a mixture of both 'X' and 'Y'. Thus, creating a new life being either a female, 'XX' or a male, 'XY'. The question I ask myself is whether nature or nurture has more of a profound influence on the gender difference when tasked with parenthood. A generally accepted standard definition of each would be 'nature', where the biological factors or the genetic composition is a far greater influence on a human personality than 'nurture', which impact is far more due to one's upbringing or life experiences. My contention is that nurture has to be a stronger case than any determination from embryonic or DNA material. Although our bodily compositions are very similar, it is the environment around us that builds such a unique memory of experiences that we all use in our approach in times when we communicate with others. Is it that boys will be boys being conditioned to think in that way? Or where girls just accepted, they were always going to be as sweet as pie. Being conditioned that the gender forms are so different can manifest in how men and women interact in one of life's episodes. This one. The journey to parenthood!

My starting proposition has been greatly influenced having picked up and now read a few times the book by Dr John Gray, *Men Are from Mars and Women Are from Venus*.

I cannot recall how I stumbled across his publication or who suggested it, but his 'teachings' were right up my street. For many years, I had struggled with putting my big size ten foot in many a situation with the women in my life. It became fairly evident that I would hear the messages communicated but incorrectly decipher the content. Hard as I tried to give the support as required, invariably, my actions inflamed the situation and ended in disaster. Clearly, my period of early nurturing was way out of kilter.

From his observations, I quickly grasped his use of a clever metaphor where a man's and a woman's distinct personality reactions to certain situations are so glaringly different; it is as if we surely must originate from two distinct planets.

Paraphrasing, his conjecture was to explain that these separate human races were living independently on two other planets. Mars and Venus. Through time and by some chance of fate, both ended up on another planet called Earth, where they decided to conjoin on that heavenly sphere living for the rest of time in abject harmony! (On the basis that we all wake up and smell the paint as to Earth's fragility and that it won't end up as a scorched surface within a hundred years).

When males were together in their own domain (with no interaction with women), they spoke another language and acted in a very archetypical way. The emotions displayed appeared less obvious and gregarious but remained deeply felt nonetheless. Females, on the other hand, interacted differently in their sole group. They were very happy to share outwardly to all and sundry how they felt with any other planetary being (a fellow Venetian) that would be happy to listen. A grouping of residents on Venus that was endless. These humanoids were much better at airing their thoughts in a more public manner and were quite vocal as to their emotional state. There was no urge to keep a stiff upper lip, to not divulge what assistance they needed, or to hold back on sharing.

Not to steal any thunder whereupon it is later considered, but as a taster, the different reactions from even the news that conception had been achieved provide a very different retort. Those that have their roots from Venus, warp to a state of hysteria, moving up five gears and exhibiting an uncontrollable glow. The excitement needs to be divulged to everyone as Venetians do to extreme detail. It is a very visible outpouring of love and affection. On the contrary, Martians (including myself) do not see that it is necessary to make any grand announcement. Such a benign response, however, is invariably misconstrued as being ambivalent by Venetians, which is not the case. It's just that Martians portray a more measured and controlled response to the experience of childbirth and bringing up a baby. To many Martians, it is just as rewarding and humbling. The one exception to the new parents 'childbirth glow' is if there is a simultaneous practical element to the announcement, such as getting the photocopier to work to print out copious copies of the sixteen-week scan picture. A Martian may actually show some form of outward emotion on the successful completion of a task well done.

The change in the relationship dynamics from the decision to start a family is arguably an adult life scenario that cannot be eclipsed. There is no wonder when either parent advocates their approach is the best. (Not forgetting the default mannerism of the Martians is to retain the happy equilibrium by remembering that either 'A happy wife leads to a happy life' or, as written down for the directions to a pub toilet 'men to the left as women are always right'). This could equally relate to either the practical application of raising a child or any emotional signatures flying around.

It is therefore advanced, not as an expert, but as personal observations, moving into parenthood leads to an incredible number of moments that could be funny, hysterical, sad, frustrating, or even cringe-worthy. This tale is one of a torchbearer that attempts to analyse the male gender experience of parenting from conception through parts of the first year of a newborn baby's life. Relying mostly on these experiences, it is not to say some situations have been embellished but still remain quite plausible. It is also not the intention to suggest any form of misogyny is behind any of the situations described. Indeed, men, arguably without exception, have the greatest respect for any birth mum and are mesmerised as to what their bodies go through for the sake of sustaining the next generation.

This perspective ends as a dedication to all those dads–the unsung heroes that have to put up with a lot of misunderstanding from the mums albeit some may have been created by themselves. To have kept on smiling with teeth locked shut, avoiding the war of words when Venetians have an outburst of contradiction at the man's approach being perceived as not quite up to the mark as required in their world.

Chapter 1
Coming of the Dawn

Parenting differences really commence pre-birth. It is not about launching into how Martians appreciate how great practicing making babies can be but the drop-dead fear of how couples react to the new era that is to commence in about forty weeks' time.

Men do not consider any planning as to the potential birth date from conception. I am not sure whether most women do either. However, recognising my conjecture of the alpha Venetian mum, it is a most vital consideration. The sense of when to try and conceive is not necessarily a binary calculation, but the alphas merely drop a hint that there is a 'preferential period' that would, to coin a phrase, tick all the boxes. To alphas and in no order of priority, an ideal time would first coincide with their birth sign. In my fictitious alpha mum scenario, let's assume a star sign Leo being between 21 July and 20 August. Why? Well, it may be obvious to like-minded alphas, but being the same star sign, one would start to build up a birth tradition starting with her. The next criterion could be more of a seasonal wish, i.e., to have a summer baby. By this, the outfits could then be purchased with a more enriched pallet of colours and comprising of the latest designer clothes. This underlying agenda is, of course, to show off 'The Special One' to the world.

All Venetians would have a utopian dream as to how becoming a mum would be like. The birth would be a short labour, no pain, during the day (so no grimacing of the face and not during the witching hours of the night), and with the delivery bed by a picture window so that the beautiful blue sky punctuated with fluffy clouds could be in full view. The man in this situation would not murmur a word but would be thinking, *Dream on, that will never happen.*

This undertone of birth planning is therefore a foreign concept to most Martians. On their planet, the thoughts that flow through are merely just a case of let's rock on and get the job done once the decision is taken to move forward with a family. There is no dream of what may or may not happen at birth. It's all rather too early. As to which month of the year and whose birth sign (if you believe such hocus pocus has any element of science behind it as to determine the personality of some new life): Pah, who cares? The main overture that a Martian considers is the hope and dream that conception requires frequent attempts and the cause is mighty lengthy!

Any approach to manipulating as to when the birth would happen is a relatively modern social change. It was very different up to the nineteen-sixties. It was a case of marriage first and no pre-nuptial sex for most. As such, there was more mysticism as to whether or not a man's tackle was in good working order or the inner working of a woman's baby plumbing facility. Depending on the length of time when couples had met and the period of engagement, come the day of marriage, it was very difficult to contain the most natural urge known to homo sapiens. As soon as the vows were taken, it was forward to the proverbial honeymoon, for all systems go like an express train with no stops.

In the case of my parents, they had wed in early September. Although I am sure no encouragement was necessary, their honeymoon just happened to coincide with a rain-drenched week in Woolacombe, Devon. The other small matter we now take for granted is the proficiency of contraception. A ninety-nine percent success rate of 'the barrier method' was a mere pipe dream in the nineteen-fifties. Needless to say, the reusable rubber sock, which owes itself more to a bicycle innertube, did not hold up during the ferocity of the honeymoon. Nine months later, my brother was the end result.

Whilst this is a 'fly on the wall' embellishment of a plausible situation with my parents, I recently found actual evidence of this problem of infancy contraception contained within a memoir passage of an auntie. Her paraphrased recollection was thus:

"I knew I was pregnant when I left Littlehampton after a rainy week staying in the Guest House. People always laughed (fellow Venetians, as would be deemed too much information by Martians) when I told them I became pregnant in Littlehampton. I wonder why! Naturally, we were miserable about this unwanted circumstance as far too early after our wedding. I wrote to the pharmaceutical chemists responsible for the faulty goods (the rubber socks). It did no good, but it made me feel better. The excuse was that their goods had been stored in too cold a place (I assume like tyres!)."

There is something poetic about how family planning was in the past, akin to Russian Roulette. Conception was out of love, passion and in the hands of a higher being. Or how good the 'vulcuners' were in producing the thinnest of the sheath that could stand the test of use. It was a common occurrence and generally accepted as a sign of the times. After the shock of realising pregnancy had occurred, it was a matter of brushing oneself down and getting on with matters as they presented themselves. I sort of envy that generation, as it was not pre-subscribed as to when. As a culture, the mystic in the creation of new life has now silently slipped away without our realisation as to what has been lost.

I digress. In this portrayal of such planning from an alpha mum, this would have a meteoric impact on any Martian that happened to be in full employment. It would call for diarised events to be minimised so that readiness and availability were assured as to when a peak performance was required. To align with Leo counting backwards would be around November or December. Not the best period to make your apologies for those seasonal drinkies in the pub and office parties. This was all to maximise the chances of success in a relatively short but intense four-week window in staging the horizontal bedroom Olympics.

As such, the scene is set for the alpha Venetian to meticulously plan and follow any interventions or advice to determine the ovulation window so that the attainment of the overarching goal of a baby falling under the Leo star sign is achievable.

The thoughts of most men in this situation would be to drift towards how it would be played out in practice. When would it be known that the moment had arrived? Whilst the most natural coupling known to animals, with such scrutiny, how would such a Martian deal with the pressure to perform when procreation was not about passion and romance but an exacting timetable with no room for failure to meet the dreams of their chosen Venetian?

Contrary to the outward air of confidence built by many of the habitants of Mars, we have been able to learn how to hide our feelings and the fog of anxiety that can well up in such a situation where failure may occur. The fear that fills us with dread and how one would cope with that look. Most Martians know that look. That look from the other planet dweller that your performance had been so underwhelming you were undeserving to be in her presence and should hop foot back to Mars. Venetians therefore can be insensitive in such a situation as to the stress put on Martians as they do not openly discuss their fears and tribulations. I have seen many a film portraying such an awkward situation where the Martian is interrupting his day-to-day routine to get back to his home bedroom for his ejaculate to be delivered in all sorts of comedic ways only to draw a blank.

The pressure valve of a love-making situation casts me back to my student days. I first shared a room with Pete in Ilford, East London, which was the home of a single mother of amazing stinginess proportions, having her own stay-at-home children also there in a typical suburban semi-mock Tudor residence of the 1930s. The location was not too far from the Polytechnic (as it was then), where a short hop on the number 123 bus delivered me to the campus. To say that the house rules had to be strictly adhered to and centred around the landlady spending as little money as possible out of our monthly room rental would be an understatement. The lodging arrangement included breakfast and an evening meal but no lunch. Being an apprehensive nineteen-year-old, I did not notice at first, but after a couple of weeks, I observed in the recess of the stairs what must have been two hundred rolls of toilet paper.

The meals that were provided always had to be bulked up with potatoes. Suffice to say, looking in the larder, you could not see much else. The bread was rationed to one slice at breakfast. I am not sure whether Pete had the same assessment, but I was questioned as to the depth of bath water I had been using and the quantity of toilet paper after a 'number two' which the landlady thought was disappearing way too fast. Imagine that getting her facts right would entail numbering the individual sheets of toilet paper and nipping in after each use to keep a tally. She even noticed I had taken the crust of a loaf of bread one lunchtime on a return to the lodgings after a free afternoon to dip into a 'pot noodle' which clearly was against the house rules.

This particular evening, we headed off to the university halls of residence social room to catch a Woody Allen film they were showing. This was 1980, and the film from 1972 was "Everything You Always Wanted to Know about Sex." My diary was empty. Beer in hand, we sat down. To my surprise, it was quite a subdued audience given the title and the testosterone flying around the other young males in the cinema room. Yes, with the exception of one female student due to the fact all were on an engineering course, which back in nineteen-eighties Britain was normally just filled by a gathering of Martians.

The film had sections that were most bizarre. Such as an overgrown breast attacking a town and a chap that had fallen in love with a sheep dressed with a suspender belt around its arse. However, there was one sketch that really caught my imagination. Was it my empathy for the chap in what I could associate with a similar pressurised performance circumstance? In this scene Woody Allen was in the back of a Volkswagen 'Beetle' beside the most attractive woman. It clearly was to be the first time that sex was on the agenda.

So, 'Woody' was in the rear seat, but the scene switches to his brain, where there is an engine room parody akin to NASA's mission control or a nuclear submarine. There was a horseshoe arrangement with various personnel controlling the body's functions in the brain. All this was orchestrated by the swathe Burt Reynolds in a central cortex position, which I am sure today would be replaced by someone like Pierce Brosnan. I cannot recall specific tasks controlled by the operatives, but the gist was there was some person rotating the eyes to potentially commence the arousal mechanism of looking at the woman's breasts. Another person controlling the tongue and puckering up the lips to move in for a French kiss to 'up the anti-' in this love embrace.

Whilst all this was going on, 'Burt' rang down to the penis room on one of those old handheld radio mics and asked to 'get ready' as an erection may be called for any moment. This was visualised by a beam crane controlled by hard hat workers that had a steel cable attached to the hand-turning wheels in preparation for the potential change in angle. At the same time, the film switched back to the car scene, where more panting was going on and clothes were being removed. A cut back to the brain followed, which then showed Burt requesting on his mic for the 'penis room' to provide a fifteen-degree erection. The next imagery was the penis urethra itself, where Woody and others were dressed in white 'onesies' with tails, signifying they were individual sperm. It was funny to see them discussing what was to happen to them once they had to jump out and swim. In which direction, was it going to be dark, and how they need to race against each other to reach the egg?

At that moment, Burt called for a further change in angle to a forty-five-degree erection and for the sperm to ready themselves for ejaculation. The sperm hooked onto a parachute jump line as would be present in a military plane. They wished each other good luck and were ready to go. More heavy breathing in the car led to panic in the brain to say ejaculation was coming. "Everyone get ready." "Don't lose your nerve." And sperm "Go, Go, Go."

The part that got to me and other Martians in fits of raucous laughter was my future reaction, as seen by the flashback to the brain with the celebration of a job well done. There were pats on the back, champagne bottles uncorked where the personnel had their feet up on the desks, and heads rolled back smoking cigarettes. Not that I had ever smoked but recognised the sentiment as a sigh of relief that the mission had been accomplished.

I wondered if I was to be that successful, hitting the mark as and when required but without the support of Burt in my head.

Chapter 2
'Ready Steady Go'

Most men would hope the whole experience of procreation would retain some form of romance. What system could be used to know that ovulation time was approaching? Perhaps a simple semaphore system involving a pair of knickers (or preferably a thong) dangling from the bed knob on the Venetian side of the bed.

The raising of the underwear could indicate all systems are go. This would marginally retain some sexiness to the task in hand with a subtle nudge rather than 'get on board and do your best'.

Indeed, such messaging could also include a colour-coded system. White or black could be the signal of a marginal ovulation zone. Get ready, it's still worth a good try just in case the ovulation date was incorrect, and after all, sperm can last quite a long time. A change to red underwear would be the signal for the arrival of a three-day ovulation peak period but also a subliminal message that whatever the man thought would be on his agenda now has to be dropped.

The question that occurs to Martians is, whilst they accept the premise conception remains a matter of chance, do you remain stoic in that belief or surrender to the detailed planning and interventions that you know are coming, particularly from an alpha Venetian? Certainly, if the former casual approach is spotted, hellfire and brimstone would descend. So, when the idea is floated that what would be a fantastic approach is to augment a 'Conception Action Plan' (as shall be abbreviated to CAP, a form of barrier method to halt pregnancy, which in this situation is clearly off the agenda!), a Martian would have great difficulty in suppressing the urge to roll one's eyes or look to the heavens as if to do a quick ceiling inspection. We can only imagine what would be next.

The science of ovulation and the myths as to what is added to such a CAP are a myriad of conflicting character differences between the genders. The research stage used to consist of a bookshelf of material gathered by the Venetian. Building up to a pile of literature that becomes a health hazard from the sheer weight of preconceptual do's and do nots and all you need to know about childbirth. Nowadays, it's 'Google'. A wonderful tool and aid to reference any and all information by the discerning Venetian. Martians do have small secret ventures on the subject, but this is to reconfirm what is being said just to be mindful of any wriggle room on any of the suggested requirements.

It is no surprise to hear that the primary requirement is the 'have sex' bit. Whoopee dee, one would say, but actually, it provides a myriad of intensity in the minds of either partner. How much, how often, or even when? On a Google search came the following:

"In general, every other night around the time of ovulation helps increase your chance of getting pregnant," Goldfarb says. Sperm can live up to five days inside your body. The best suggestion is to have sex regularly *when you're ovulating and* (my emphasis) *when you're not.*

What great news! Who would have thought the guidance was to keep at it all the time? Oh boy, Mars dwellers, eat your heart out. Christmas, birthdays, anniversaries, and the weekend away have now just been scheduled altogether.

To focus the mental capacity of Martian men who are about to enter the conception phase, it is arguably not beyond an alpha Venetian requirement to insist on the use of a very visual flip chart. (As one would expect them to consider for any of life's major events, such as a wedding.) In such a scenario, five coloured pens to establish various priorities could be lined up on the easel. Most people would have thought the front hanging A2 sheet should provide sufficient space to cover all the circumstances. As shall be revealed later, this assumption is as close to no chance as one could get.

So having established the primary requirement, 'have sex', the supplemental conception requirements need to be assessed. With a glee…at first, the man googles on the sly to confirm what he himself would like to deliver up on the old flip chart: *Have sex every day during the fertile window.*

Most genders would tend to agree that what constitutes 'regular' participation does in itself take on a different meaning as to whether conception aligns at the time of youthful vigour or when life moves into a more maturing sexual landscape. This is when the language of the planets as to how many attempts can diverge. And for this reason, the next entry for the CAP was to *monitor ovulation.* A free-for-all is not on the agenda but focused periods of strenuous activity. Alpha mums would sharpen their pencils to plot an ovulation chart in the CAP as accurately as possible as to when the right time for a really concerted effort needs to be planned. This would give the foremost judgment as to the most likely time for that old egg to roll down the fallopian tube giving the maximum opportunity to conceive.

The next part of the Google Search suggested when to have sex. "Have it in the morning, as research shows that a man's sperm count is higher at this time, so take advantage of it!"

Wow, an open door for the men except for considering any negative ramifications. Could one really diarise morning sessions for the whole week when having to get up at the crack of dawn for a commute before a hard day's employment shift? It could then quickly become a conception plan nightmare! In common with other Martians, some have instilled a work ethic where any task required by the employer deserves our fullest attention, even if this conflicts with ovulation time. A Venus woman sees it differently. If that's what the CAP requires, then there is no debate.

When a call to action is required, of course, all the ovulation planets would be aligned to coincide with the most immovable morning meeting. Typically, Martians also have a high commitment to attention to detail that manifests into becoming preoccupied with the task at hand. So, when being greeted with the news that with a bit of a wink and smile ovulation time had arrived and a morning lift-off was a go, it would not always feel like a total clean sweep of good news.

The man's solution would be:

"That's fine. But we would need to get down to business before 5:30 am, as I need to leave the house within the hour from conception countdown so I am not late for work."

The house would grow eerily silent and accompanied by the piercing glare of a lioness before she steps out in a stealthy manner to attack a gazelle:

"I think you have your priorities wrong, my dear. I can't possibly wake up at that time. You will just have to go to work later and make your excuses."

It is a wonder how men and women ever procreate, as this situation exemplifies the differences between the gender home planets. In the man's world, he didn't know ovulation was going to arrive that night (Perhaps he should have taken more notice of the ovulation graphs!) having already planned that very important meeting in good faith. He does not want to let the team down. He also thinks my job brings in the cash for both of us and is one of the reasons why we are now in this position to create a family. Surely, reason enough to heed a request for a 5:30 am start.

The Venetian view would be wholly divergent in the thought process. He knew ovulation day was getting close as the cycle was plotted and recorded on the chart. If he took more notice of what we (The royal we) had agreed, then he would have been completely aware of when ovulation may be occurring. It is his job to have factored this into planning his meeting so as to avoid any potential conflict. Morning procreation sessions would be likely and therefore the absolute priority. If his work required a meeting with the chance of a clash, it was his responsibility to ensure his absence would not be missed in the morning, or at the very least a strategy regarding excuses for being delayed should have already been prepared.

Thus, for the Venetian, as this situation was seen to be wholly avoidable, there was no reason for a compromise to get up earlier than needed as this problem had been created outside the CAP.

Faced with this 'gentle' reminder, the more informed or tactically astute of men would not continue with an exchange when such a battle would be inevitably lost and just confirm through teeth gripped:

"Okay then, I will go in later."

This is the Martian solution, remembering the saying 'Happy Wife, Happy Life'. Should there be a thought of compromise, I hear you asking. Well, if the Venetians and Martians had stayed on their own planets and mastered the art of asexual reproduction, then maybe. However, as each 'race' decided to abandon their home planet for the sake of togetherness, then 'not a chance' as far as the dominant being was concerned, which clearly in this situation was the Venetian.

Having conceded it was now the case of limiting the embarrassment of a late work arrival. Could time be taken off the normal routine? Most Martians' time management for the morning get-up-and-leave routine is already quite efficient. There could only be marginal gains. Shaving at bedtime could cut (excuse the pun) possibly four minutes from the average thirty-five minute routine. What about a further small gain by pre-toasting bread and leaving it in the fridge overnight? Perhaps also making the cup of tea fully loaded with milk so both could be slipped into the microwave in the morning to be reheated simultaneously as one dresses with a shirt, trousers, and tie all pre-laid out on the floor of the kitchen.

All the above could give a reasonable efficacy against the norm but remains unlikely to gain sufficient time, as one knew there was no chance of the said Venetian rising earlier than needed for any Martian work commitment. The only alternative, in this situation, for a Martian would be to turn their attention to assess what excuses could be made but at the same time be perceived as credible.

The usual traffic hold-ups on the commute route reason have become the new standard in the book of office excuses, surpassing the note from mum or wife. "Tommy has an upset stomach and can't come in." It also didn't help that when others proffered such an excuse, it was usually treated with cynicism that they just overslept and an easy one to discredit with advice they should just get up thirty minutes earlier. Why shouldn't you just be able to tell the truth to your colleagues?

"Sorry, I am late. I didn't check the ovulation graph my wife had prepared that identified the next cycle's peak zone was today. I also admit to not paying attention to my own personal checklist, which states sperm swim faster in the mornings. As such, I was called upon to stand to attention and do my duty in the morning, making the appropriate delivery before I was able to leave the house, and hence my delay."

Mmm. Nope, it is just not possible to be that brazen. Quickly going through more inane reasons for the lateness of his attendance in his mind ('The car wouldn't start', 'alarm clock didn't go off' or 'a tyre had a puncture'), the back pocket excuse became:

"The heating pump seized, which led to a buildup in pressure that needed me to close the system down by turning off the stopcock in the verge, which was buried. I am surprised I made it in before the end of the meeting."

The last part he thought would be a nice touch.

Contrary to the view of women, sex for men is not just a matter of mechanics but does need an element of saucy invitation. Greeted with morning breath in a yawn to signify time to hop on board is not the greatest of encouragement to procreate. One should be very careful as to what is consumed the night before and whether both had had similar amounts of the said substance. Ignoring for the moment stale alcohol or a smoker's exhalation, one has to single out garlic. Some like a little of the vegetable and others copious amounts. Without equal quantities consumed by him and her, it's just not a morning aphrodisiac, is it? Nor is the Martians' inbuilt guilt of leaving late for work and that important meeting arranged in good faith.

So sets the scene of a stressful conception encounter brought about by having to comply with the CAP. As the time lengthens from the appearance of the starting pistol, the stress continues, as for once a quick-fire trigger mechanism is not operating. The tension builds with the Martians' face twitching to enable involuntary glances over to the clock on the bedside table, thinking why aren't we there yet? Eventually, yes, eventually a dribble occurs. With a sigh of relief and a quick escape down those stairs to pick up the clothes laid out on the floor at the same time as whacking on the microwave for the pre-prepared tea and toast his thoughts turn to why can't we just go back to the old-fashioned way of pot luck.

In part relating to the importance of the man's performance and also an alpha woman's desire to conceive for the chosen due date, it is best next to consider any improvements that could be included within the CAP. This would relate to either increasing the sperm count or motility. As one of the many organisations dealing with advice on the internet comes this. It's important you prepare *your body and*

adjust your lifestyle to maximise your chances of conception.
Strive for a healthy body weight.

My Martian metaphorical cave for matters of stress, anxiety, or standard old 'I have had enough' is a bike. Depending on the severity of the self-doubt attack, this could be peddling for hours, even days if allowed. So, no chance of carrying a shed load of too much weight even after a wayward binge drinking or eating session. However, for those men whose cave is either down the pub or to take solace in comfort eating slumpt on a sofa, this would be more of an exacting lifestyle change. This could lead to a vocal intervention from Venetians to suggest more positive health actions are needed, accompanied by a tongue-whip lashing.

"Don't just sit there, go and walk the dog. And I mean for at least an hour at a quick pace with a jog around the park."

Or:

"You don't care that you need to play your part in trying to conceive. It's alright for you to go down to the pub with your mates and watch the football, but what about keeping healthy and sitting with me to watch the soaps instead. (uninteresting dramas for most Martians!)"

The next item on any CAP list from the research would be to *keep cool,* where it would be noted that *men have a higher sperm count when their genitals are kept at a cooler temperature. So, stay away from hot tubs, hot showers, and tight-fitting underwear.*

Hot tubs have never been on my agenda, but a fitness club pleasure has always been the sauna or a hotter shower than at home. This creates a potential moral dilemma for anyone as to whether one could pull off a sneaky treatment without revealing such an indiscretion. It turns on the ability of

Martians to brazenly lie when challenged as to the correct version of the truth. Problem. Our facial muscles are not designed the same as on Venus, even when we are not guilty. They always appear uncontrollable and not connected to our brain when glared at and asked to fully engage with a Venetian stare.

It's a similar situation as happens in childhood when asked by your parents if you have had a biscuit without asking and, unbeknown, there is a ring of crumbs around the mouth. Most Martians always have an air of guilt around them. I am no exception when, as a mere three-year-old, this happened to me. Shouldering the blame for nearly setting alight my parent's house for half a century until my brother eventually coughed up the truth.

In the sixties, central heating was unheard of. The primary source of fuel was a coal fire in the hearth of the main front room. When this could not raise the temperature to sufficient warmth, a supplemental source was normally required. In this tale, it was an electric heater having two coiled bars in which a current passed through. There were two settings. On and off. Needless to say, there was scant regard for health and safety at that time. The only protection against the highly dangerous and flammable source of heat from the super-heated coils was an open steel guard. This 'safety feature' attained the same heat as the coils and was soon to understand that when you push something wooden with wool strands at one end, it is surprising as to the ease one could set this alight if shoved towards the electric fire elements.

On this one occasion, my brother (who was three years older than myself) and I were in the front room on a cold autumn morning dressed in our vests and underpants. My mother was quite prone to distraction and, as usual, engaged in a lengthy conversation with a complete stranger on the doorstep. The chap turned out to be a Tupperware salesman with his products in a suitcase. Rather than doing what most people would consider normal, she didn't say, 'no thanks, I must get back to my children'. Instead, the time lag was sufficient for my brother to decide it would be a good idea to stick the washing-up mop into the electric fire to see what would happen. It didn't take long, but long enough to set it alight and hand it to me. Mum was still oblivious, but my scheming brother sent me to the front entrance, where she was still entertaining the salesman with the same inane monologue. Looking back, I could see the funny side, as even I could recall resembling an Olympic marathon athlete with a flaming torch running to light the game's flame.

Both the salesman and mum stamped on the said flaming mop, whereupon I was chastised. This episode was regurgitated and became a childhood legend until he revealed with a smirk that it was him that handed me the triumphant mop many years later.

As I had a look of guilt and didn't point the finger at my brother, the assumption was it must have been the story provided by him. It is always a timely reminder that if one cannot even look innocent when not guilty, the notion that having had a hot sauna breaking the 'keep cool' regulation in the CAP was a non-starter.

Alpha Venetians wishing to conceive would give further examples as to what the 'keep cool' regulation demanded of their male counterpart. Possibly loose-fitting pants were appropriate. I assume those monstrous old-fashioned briefs, which were only a notch below a parachute. My dad used to have many a pair. As children, they were large enough to frequent our heads during the mad half hour at bedtime to resemble Egyptian Pharaohs.

The matter of keeping the genitals cool could also take on an added dimension if a man, like me, has their metaphorical cave as a bike or any other 'crown jewels' hugging clothing with a similar high intensity of activity. For myself, this would manifest and be clearly visible on my return from such exercise, by dripping sweat from under the helmet centrifugally drawn in from the head and nose down to the chin and forming into a pool of water big enough for any child to don their boots, thinking it's a puddle to jump in. Undoing the straps and taking off the lid would always bring a further splattering of moisture, akin to a shaggy dog expunging water from a dip in a river.

Normally, this would be met by an "Urghh…how disgusting." Instead, this greet would exhibit no hesitation in the Venetian running up to any spandex bib shorts with a pack of frozen vegetables in hand and pressing them without mercy into the crotch. A situation with the hope that a neighbour could not see the prospective mum on her knees holding out the cold press towards the male undercarriage or hear the inevitable high-pitched whimper.

This new post-cycle 'keep cool' cool-down routine, albeit a step too far, is another example of a Martian staying tight-lipped for the sake of continuing good relations.

There would be no difference between the sexes aligning to a no-smoking or drug ban, as their negative impact on sperm or conception is well documented. But that is nowadays and a subject that would need to be revisited after the birth. But what of any do's and don'ts regarding food and drink?

The first consideration would be the quantity of liquids to be consumed each day. Men find it extremely difficult to find the time to drink the recommended 8 to 10 cups per day. Change this to beer, cider, or lager, and this would be no problem. Not quite sure how this would determine the quality of sperm and an increased chance of conceiving in accordance with the CAP but falling back to males' default position, 'Anything for a quiet life', most Martians would give it their all to comply.

Should there be an absolute requirement during conception for no alcohol to pass your lips? This would be a tough ask unless, of course, you are one of the handful of Martians that are tea-total. Such an aspiration was not quite the same in the past, as many, for different reasons, took the pledge. Some out of financial necessity. Others had known of bad experiences in partaking of the devil's brew. It was not a problem for my grandparents, as they never touched a drop, and clearly the limited alcohol my parents consumed had no impact on sprouting four children.

Whilst accepted that not avoiding or strictly limiting alcohol intake could reduce fertility, this does not factor in the relaxant quality of a pint of beer or glass of wine to the Martian at such a stressful time put on his performance. Sure, medically, alcohol is not a proven reducing tension drug, but oh boy sitting in your 'special' chair or place looking at that glass of this particular guilty pleasure brings a state of calmness immeasurable against other relaxants. Eating an apple or drinking lemonade just does not have the same impact!

Again, this is one of those odd occasions when a man would go to hell and back to disprove or provide leverage that a reasonably restrained alcohol intake is not that bad. It is true that one can always find some contradictory advice on the Web, and this time is no different. One of those that popped up fortuitously stated that one or two alcoholic drinks per day are actually okay for men. It was only when more than fourteen mixed drinks in a week or five or more drinks in a two-hour time frame were consumed did testosterone levels or sperm count become affected. Oh yes, happy days are here again. Even if having a crafty one or two of the banned beverages, one could countenance any perceived finger-pointing as to a failed conception attempt. However, the smart Martian would not divulge this crucial thread of research openly, as he would know any attempt to introduce such evidence in the face of the total alcohol ban would, of course, "Not stand up in court, Guv."

Having thought the CAP had been completed as far as any direct impact on the Martians' lifestyle, it was a shock as to the depth of dutiful support that was now called for, as revealed by the next A2 sheet. 'Dietary changes that are to be introduced.'

Whether or not 'super foods' impact a great deal on sperm fertility Venetians have an expectation that their men would be happy to participate, demonstrating their unwavering support.

Apparently, marginal gains can be made by including in the diet asparagus, Brussels sprouts, eggs, bananas, dark chocolate, Brazil nuts and walnuts. No problem except wondering whether any gaseous expulsions after such a diet would have an impact on the rarefied conception atmosphere of the bedroom. Pumpkin seeds are a good source to increase zinc levels, as they are one of the best minerals for male fertility. A scenario when the decision is made to push for a baby would be the breakfast, where there would be an unseen morning weigh-in of the pumpkin seeds to confirm strict adherence.

Meals should also focus on a Mediterranean diet and steer away from those bad fat pleasures, including bacon, sausages, and full-fat cheese. This change is very hard for many males who find it difficult to get excited with salads, including tomatoes, olives, oysters, and any foodstuffs swimming in a pool of oily vinaigrette dressing.

The thought of how to keep the woman happy at the same time of retaining small guilty pleasures is at the fore of any Martian. For some men who have the general responsibility for the weekly shop, there is an opportunity to sneak in the odd bottle of wine, beer, or even a mini-pack of pork pies. Martians do, however, understand that Venetians are as cunning as foxes having received better training on their planet. So it would be of no surprise that there would be a border bag check on the doorstep. Not just to ensure that the correct food stuffs had been purchased but that there were no signs of contraband. If you know that gaze, when you have been caught red-handed doing anything you ought not to you would appreciate the sentiment if a bottle of wine was found in the bottom of the bag. This situation does not exclude the possibility of a counter plan where one could attempt to stealthily hide a banned substance by delaying its carriage from the far reaches of the car boot by a few minutes when you thought the coast was clear.

A major lifestyle change that may assist conception is reducing stress. Consider a situation when a Martian is classified as a workaholic. It would be unhelpful and a self-defeating suggestion if a Venetian's radar picks up that his focus on his career is unduly increasing his lack of ability to relax during the period of the CAP. Martians would say to work hard, be committed, be conscientious, and always be diligent is a typical characteristic. As such, the man needs to ensure his demeanour remains and not radiating too much workplace pre-occupation as he would surely be caught out! This is the trait that appears more likely with the male gender and is not fully understood by the mothers-to-be. This is quite ironic, as women are far better at multi-tasking, so why not assume men can cope just as well with work pressures simultaneous with their contribution towards a successful conception?

The majority of men are pretty clued up when they cross that home threshold after a day's work. They must be mindful of not taking work home with them. Both physical or not to remain immersed in thought (unless part of a cunning plan to delay or not participate in an undesirable task!). There is, shall we say normally, a window of opportunity to gather oneself either as you walk down the path to the front door or turn the engine off in the car before you switch into happy couple mode and for the greater good. This is particularly relevant during the CAP period, where positive readiness is a pre-requisite for any planned conception activity expected that evening, the following morning, or heaven forbid, during a weekend. A lesson learnt through time was it was futile to leave oneself exposed to a lengthy discussion of the day's events rather than a limited exchange, throwing in the odd comment being no longer than two words.

"How was your day, darling? I hope not too stressful." A likely question posed.

The man's CAP period repertoire to demonstrate a non-stressful work period would be 'Okay', 'Good', 'No problems' and my particular favourite that covers all eventualities without giving anything away as to how the day really went, "Fine."

Another CAP requirement would be avoiding toxins, which in reality is always preferable at any time. Ingesting harmful substances that may affect the quality of both sperm and embryo would be absolutely soul-destroying, which thankfully nowadays this risk is far less due to 'elf & safety'. It wasn't always this way.

In times past, one would not think too deeply as to the presence of any potentially harmful substance or any interventions one should take. Mask protection was not insisted upon to stop ingestion and, in most instances, a complete absence of any protective gear. Hazards were bleeding everywhere. Even sucking on the end of a proper lead pencil was pretty widespread by all budding scholars in the 1960s-1970s. For myself, this was not my only potential exposure. As a twelve-year-old lad, the Sunday school teacher used to take my brother and I under his wing. (Today, it would probably be viewed as a safeguarding issue!) It usually involved a pick up on a Saturday to his uncle's farm. My parents were very happy to see us out of their hair. Great fun was had driving tractors and sitting on either the roof or the front wing of a Land Rover as he drove along the farm tracks. On one particular afternoon, after noticing the size of pot holes akin to no man's land in WWI in the byways, we set off to an asbestos roofing factory. There was no clue sitting in the cab as to what was to greet us pulling up into their rear yard.

"Come on, lads, help me load up these broken sheets (asbestos) into the rear of the Land Rover. We are going to use them later to lay over the track holes. We will then ride over them in the 'Rover' back and forth, crushing the sheets to smaller pieces and creating particles of dust to fill the gaps," he said.

This event only happened once but makes one think. This was possibly my first but not the last contact with dodgy material. Being in attendance during the early stages of housing developments meant I had on one occasion the assignment of standing around next to radio-active second world war instrument dials in a former MoD burning ground. Latterly, within a small business start-up park, I was informed mustard gas canisters had been indiscriminately buried. Even standing in one particular farmer's field, there was potential exposure to anthrax from buried animal carcasses. Worst of all was a trail pit at a former tannery. The contamination was so bad that various bio-degradable matter was oozing out from the sides of animal carcasses and detergents to clean the leather. The smell was indescribable.

It was a godsend; my business activities were only interesting to those involved in the industry. As such, there was no threat I would have my day picked over from such experiences by my Venetian and then, having discovered the true extent of potential sperm showstoppers. As it happens, the only side-effect to my offspring was just the normal teenage attitudes.

In life, we have to make choices in a balanced way as to those interventions, which can be unduly restrictive when considering a common goal. In this instance, describing what is best to 'guarantee' fertile sperm. Exercise for a healthy lifestyle or the faintest of chances to any possible air-borne substances are such conflicts. Since COVID, the wearing of masks to assist any transfer of viruses quickly became the norm, but beforehand such protection to any number of air-borne toxins was given scant regard. So now, when you are cycling or pounding those lanes training for a marathon and passing arable fields being sprayed or that chemical factory on the edge of town, the advice would be to try and hold one's breath. Again, be careful of how much information you give on divulging the route (Just as a man would do when returning from work), particularly to an alpha Venetian as they may, next time, demand you wear a full-faced respirator and oxygen tank on your back.

Lifestyle changes required by an alpha Venetian can at times appear quite subtle when the CAP is in full swing, but no less an impact on a man's routine. Apparently, to increase the chances of conception, one should *Swap the exercise bike* for *the treadmill.* The repeated banging of the groin against the bicycle seat can damage critical arteries and nerves, so the information that was read out in detailing the CAP entry. The dilemma for any spinning fitness fiend would be whether to laugh, cry, capitulate, or resist the pressure to lose one's man cave. Any response would have to be carefully considered, which reminded me of a lesson learnt many years ago.

It was at a formal dinner setting with other senior managers on this particular away weekend. Each participant had to pick out of a hat a subject to talk about for up to five minutes. These were not to be revealed until after the main meal was finished, where over coffee and brandy each in turn had to give their spiel. My subject was Winston Churchill with an obvious theme that could be used from the quote: *Never in the field of human conflict was so much been owed by so many to so few*. Not that I knew the whole speech verbatim but relying on my recollection of the great man's performance and the words through watching over and over again my favourite historical film, 'The Battle of Britain'.

There was one particular speaker who was to demonstrate his interpretation of 'taking time out'. It was not spawned from a creative imagination but a true story. His hobby was deep-sea diving. He had an opportunity to dive into a deep-sea wreck off the coast of Cornwall. They bottled up with the oxygen and breathing apparatus, and off they went. The remains of the ship were at a depth that needed air replacement stations and a platform to wait so as not to resurface too quickly and trigger decompression sickness. All was going well on the dive until he got entangled within a small filament fishing net, which trapped him at a depth of 150 metres. He only had ten minutes of air remaining. The problem with such a net is that it is both very strong and by nature of its use: the more you struggle to get free, it becomes tighter and more entangled. The way he explained it was that it became a life-and-death situation where he wasn't able to free himself. So, he just paused for a few seconds. He took time out to reflect on how the hell he was going to get out of the situation and save himself. He stopped flapping his arms and purposefully assessed his predicament. It gave him the time needed to focus and come up with a plan to use the last remaining oxygen in his bottle to fill the artefact balloons he had on his belt (to bring finds to the surface) and attach them to the filament net. This he did so as to free the net from his body. As he cut through just beneath where he had placed the balloons, the net was dragged away from him. He only just had sufficient air to reach the oxygen replacement platform to survive to tell the tale.

You could have heard a pin drop in the room. All the raucous laughter had completely subsided as he got further into this very extraordinary and true tale. Of course, he got the accolade as to the best after-dinner speech, and who would question that?

So, Martians would do well to consider this advice in taking a few short seconds before any response to an uncomfortable request by your Venetian. Try and practice and include within your own personal 'Martian feedback training session'. In this example, the lifestyle change was 'swap from an exercise bike'. There was no mention of not using an outdoor bike in the missive. By taking those extra few seconds before opening one's mouth, the subtle wording can be assessed with ideas to prepare for any verbal exchanges that the guidance is one regarding stress on the scrotum and not necessarily the machinery that could be responsible for the squashing of the testicles.

Such a situation is a prime example of a potential Mexican stand-off between the sexes or the degree of expectation as to how far one should go with the advice. Added to the simple fact that it is very difficult for a Martian to contradict the view of any Venetian where he is continually reminded of his lesser role in giving birth and, as a result, should be more proactive in considering the request as stipulated.

In my world, cycling would have had to be less frequent to obtain the CAP concession, added to which the accomplished skill of standing on the bike pedals more frequently to keep the gonads swinging in the breeze for longer than usual.

There was a time when a lifestyle change would also need to include limiting the use of mobile phones. To provide sufficient power for a day in the early years of the analogue first-generation tools of this non-wired communication, they needed a battery the size of a brick. Smart phones of today barely last longer, but the intensity of the power to give sufficient signal strength for even the basic modem of a call or text message was extraordinary. I must confess they did make your thigh or ear very warm after five minutes of use. Scientists in Hungary apparently had a view that men who kept mobile phones switched-on in their trouser pocket or on belts have significantly lowered sperm counts and risk their fertility being cut by up to a third. Furthermore, the sperm's motility may be affected by long calls. That's the one instance of blame that could squarely be shouldered by a Venetian when she would be shouting down the phone to turn the thing off!

Like others, to support such a mobile phone beast, one could use a belt holster requiring a size as big as one used for a cowboy's six-shooter Colt 45. This accessory did not last long once the research had been uncovered. After yet another tongue whipping of epic proportions, the suggestion was:

"No phones to be stored on a belt or trouser pockets. Even when turned off."

A further Martian lesson is required so as to not continue arguing when the cause is lost. It just has the ability to push the margins further out and exponentially get worse. If a line had been drawn then and there to comply with the primary alpha requirement, that matter would have ended. Instead, by attempting to remonstrate that some latitude was in order and not to overreact, such a challenge had the effect of the ban cordon inevitably widening. Defacto, the Venetians thought what they had initially considered and suggested was already a compromise. Huff! It was now to include any bodily pockets, not to be left on the front car seat, and when at work strict adherence was expected. The latter stipulation is to be controlled at the door threshold by an office-to-home interrogation.

Having finitely prepared the foundations for a very specific birth window more often than not, nature's spell comes to the fore where all that planning comes to nothing. A conception as laid out in the CAP remained very unlikely where no spiritual wand existed to guarantee the achievement of a targeted birth day, let alone anywhere in the birth month. Quel surprise.

The final lesson for any well-informed Martian is how to deal with the inevitable fall out. There should be no obvious smugness that all those intricate interventions were a complete waste of time. You must not use the four words 'I told you so' (which will crop up time and time again!) under any circumstances, as this would just be a red rag to a bull. Be happy in the fact that the Venetian is aware that the dream did not come true, although do not expect any admission to the fact. Be grateful that you got through the process unscathed, and by luck, the continuance of harmony reigns. But of course, having remembered there is a need to keep one's eye on what is to come once conception has been successful. Mon dieu, the pregnancy phases!

Chapter 3
'Avoiding Complications'

The conception experience now seemed a distant memory in moving towards the whole purpose as to why the genders come together: to ensure the future existence of the two species. Other Martians can sympathise that the heir apparent of each and every Venetian is going to be the most important generational addition.

In the quest to uncover how one considers expert suggestions for any mitigation of potential threats to the unborn child during pregnancy, there are, of course, different approaches, and the degree of intervention one would believe is entirely reasonable from the perspective of Men (Martians) and Women. (Venetians and alpha Venetians.)

I am not for a moment suggesting any miscarriage is not a catastrophic heartache for any couple, but thankfully such horrid events remain rare. The research yielded a proportion of one to five miscarriages per hundred live births. Although not insignificant, the likelihood is sufficiently low, so it ought not to give rise to absolute hysteria at the thought that it could happen to you so long as measured precautions or lifestyle changes are taken. Considering the main pregnancy issues, we have:

- Heavy smoking
- Alcohol
- Physical trauma
- Some foods, including pineapple, sesame seeds, raw eggs, unpasteurised milk, liver, sprouted potatoes

Ironic that now sesame seeds have become the villain of the peace and not the sperm fixer. A situation not being lost on any Martian that queries if all that fuss earlier on was really quite necessary. As for the identified potential impacts, men ought now to be sufficiently skilled to digest and note what is expected. They do not believe any further prompts or reminders are necessary. This does not stop our cohabiters from Venus from overusing the adverb 'just' whenever possible, giving a constant check as to whether full compliance is being adhered to. We are aware of this Venetian characteristic from general living:

"Are all the doors locked? Can you 'just' check again?" Asked each and every night.

"Has the coffee machine been turned off? Can you 'Just' make sure?" After travelling in the car for around five minutes from the house and being asked to turn around and check.

Or

"Can you check my hair is 'just' curled completely at the back?" Having spent an hour getting every last strand hooped and pincered in the tongs.

As is the case during conception, it is obvious smoking would not be a good idea once a pregnancy has happened. You would have to be on the moon not to have seen at least one of the health information adverts on TV since the eighties that it was simply a bad idea.

One government broadcast highlighted how the human body is not designed for smoking. The parody was about a future evolutionary skeletal change to cope with this nicotine pleasure.

The advert showed a human in a horizontal position laying in a type of chaise-long chair staring into the abyss. The only activity that was possible was being able to light up a fag. The chest was akin to a stripped chicken but thinner, where the inhaled smoke did not have to go through the palaver of being exhaled via the mouth but would by osmosis disperse through the chest cavity. The index finger had disproportionally grown to one and a half times the length of the other digits to enable more efficient flicking off of the ash building up on the cigarette. The whole smoking process was accompanied by a rasping death rattle sound. The strap line being that if we did not curtail the habit, we would all end up like this. Yuk.

Did this type of approach help? Who knows, but smoking has now become pretty socially unacceptable. One would have thought no further consideration is needed, but there is the question of passive smoking.

An alignment occurs between the genres where other people are smoking in the same room or car. To the perpetrator, a simple 'don't do that' is sufficient direction. It wasn't always this clear. Back in the twentieth century, there was a basic denial as to the impact of smoking on the unborn child. Including my Nan.

Not knowing whether she continued to smoke through her pregnancy, but when visiting her home in North London, the tar staining on the front room ceiling was for all to see. Added to the brown discoloration on her index finger or the crazed dark lines within her dentures pointed towards a lifelong habit. From the strange smoking style, those in her presence would ingest more of the detritus gunk from a fag than she would draw in herself! The cigarette would be lit and brought to the side of a very rouge covered pair of lips. Being affixed firmly to the tacky surface covering with a slight droop, the inhalation draw for the nicotine would be taken for less than a second. Everyone else then received the blowout and by default had a greater participation in smoking without wanting to. From observing such a technique, one had to ponder as to what was the point of smoking in that way if only to take a sip of the mild drug for all that cost and effort.

Now passive smoking only remains a potential hazard when walking down a street, in any public space, or sitting outside to have food and beverages. For Martians to chastise, the offending smoker remains a simple derivative of distance from where you are. The rule of thumb is that no smokers should be sitting on the same bench or at the table. On Venus, this is not accepted as sufficient where an intervening empty set of furniture is a minimum requirement.

It wasn't long until the new distance rules were to be tested. (Latterly similar to the COVID epidemic rules regarding mixing in public.) There is an expectation that the male will defend the cordon with any means necessary. Imagine a lovely sunny afternoon by the river after a long period of dull weather. Naturally, everyone had the same idea, and the outside seating area was rammed to the hilt at the pub. Not that everyone these days lights up at every social opportunity, but one of the few couples that still had the need would always be on the next table.

Martians have a distaste for confrontation over such matters where they believe the pregnant partners' requirement can be a little overzealous. That is, no desire to provide a cautionary word if some person was smoking within their range having a preference to continue with their chosen pint of amber nectar of either ale, cider, or lager in peace. When both beings cohabited on earth, Martians were given the distinct impression that Venetians were the less violent and volatile of the two species. Make them pregnant or give them a family, and it then becomes a fallacy.

Knowing that the female expected his full and unconditional support, you can imagine the scenario:

"Look, the thing is, my wife (Note not the Martian) has carried out research, and passive smoking is known to have a potential effect on the unborn child. I know the pub is very busy today but would you mind smoking further away please," he would say.

"You got to be joking, mate. F*k off! There are no tables spare, and there are no rules that say I cannot smoke anywhere in public. You move," was the response.

This is when a Martian would like the Earth to swallow him up as the full Venetian glare treatment switches to him.

"So, what are you going to do about it?" She asks.

"Well, I kind of agree with his point of view that he has just as much right to sit and smoke at his table, so perhaps we should do the moving instead to keep the peace," the Martian would say in a subdued manner now with his head pointing down and looking at his feet, ensuring no eye contact is made.

No words are needed to hear what the thoughts of the woman would be about what is regarded as a spineless climb-down with no action. The lesson learnt here for Martians is to avoid a similar situation again. From this point forward, he carefully plans any outings where contact with the general populous is unlikely. This leads to spending more time in their own garden until the baby arrives than they ever thought was possible.

It is amazing how much grief starts and ends with alcohol. Whatever the amount consumed, and even when you do not drink yourself and are surrounded by those who do, the relationship conflict that arises is second to none. Men not being biologically required for this stage of the birth journey provides a dilemma to their psyche when a request comes in that a full alcoholic ban remains to demonstrate 'we are in this together'. Considering with a pint of lager in the one hand and a Cointreau chaser in the other, to what degree of abstinence should Martians follow? Having been here before during the pre-conception stage, the right decision would be to continue with a 'visible' ban but hold on to the idea of morphing on the odd occasion into a sly drinker. Bring on the deflection technique Martians have honed through the centuries.

"Oh, you look tired, darling," he said.

"Do I?" She would respond.

"Yeah, I think you ought to go to bed early."

"Are you going to join me?" She would enquire.

"I will be up shortly, darling. I just need to finish some work before I come up."

Thus creating the opportunity to partake in a crafty alcoholic brew with the knowledge that the Venetian would likely be asleep by the time the boards of the stairs were trodden.

The working Martians would always have an opportunity for a few beers when away on business, which of course would be entirely plausible to become more often. Other potential situations could be a club night or indeed the arrangement of a least one 'lads' weekend away in the period of pregnancy.

Having dealt with the main topics regarding issues during the pregnancy journey, Venetians would more often than not consider anecdotal myths just as seriously.

Exercise is at the top of the agenda. This myth provides a dichotomy for Venetians between doing sufficient to keep the pre-pregnancy figure in good stead and the acceptance that somewhere along the nine-month journey the body just 'ain't' going to be the same. A very delicate situation therefore arises for the male partner and how to respond when asked, 'How do I look?', 'Have I still kept my figure?' or 'Do you still fancy me?' (Which is quite ironic when dealing with the final myth that could cause a miscarriage). After the fifth repeated conversation, every Martian exhausted ways of being diplomatic without being pulled up on the response as being too benign. This is the situation all men fear. How honest to be when quizzed:

"It's alright. I don't mind. You can tell me what you really think."

Venetian envy can occur when comparing the shape and what is or isn't drooping compared to other prospective mums. With this in mind, a dilemma can arise as to when is it too late to stop exercise completely prior to the pending birth. Consider a body conscious mum-to-be who, in this scenario, is a fitness instructor. It wouldn't occur to her to change her routine in the gym or to halt the lessons even in the final stages of pregnancy. Let's set a scene of a Pilates class just prior to giving birth. All females in a non-air-conditioned dance studio.

"Swing those arms one more time please," said the instructor.

"Come on, pick those feet up and now crouch in the bunny hop position."

And with her leading the class came an awkward moment.

"Oooooops, my waters seem to have broken. Class dismissed. I need to get to the hospital and deliver this baby."

With such an instructor, the class would not be at all surprised that she just picked up her gym bag, got in the car, and drove herself to the maternity ward to give birth.

As a known myth, males would just enquire to please let common sense prevail. Do not get hung up that there may be more wobbly bits where there shouldn't be during the pregnancy, but really, just don't leave it too late in the pregnancy journey!

Another myth is stress. This is all around every individual, whether pregnant or not. If stress was a direct cause of miscarriage, humankind could not have been sustained. Relationships are not always Adam and Eve prancing around in sheer delight within the Garden of Eden. Both the birth mother and partner approach stressful situations from different viewpoints, and misunderstandings are likely to happen. Even from our humble beginnings, if the man hunter-gatherer had returned empty-handed from a hunting expedition, chastising him would elevate stress for both and leave no chance of a baby in transit surviving:

"I have been sitting here in this cold and damp cave. You convinced me this was the best home on Rock Quarry Street. All I do is live in fear with the threat of being eaten by a sabre tooth tiger, and you haven't brought back even a mushroom for me to eat. You're a useless waste of space."

The hot topic as to the degree of sexual activity that may be acceptable during pregnancy is a myth that quickly becomes a subject that no party is willing to discuss. This is where knowing your partner is vital and, of course, 'how far' one is allowed or prepared to go in beating the sexual myth. Albeit this may change if the baby is overdue, where a further misconception rears its head that sex helps with the breaking of the woman's amniotic water. Under normal circumstances, unabated continuance of sexual activity would be music to most men's ears. However, now faced with a belly the size and look of a tortoiseshell, the request to 'please hop on board' is not greeted with the same enthusiasm. Sexual attractiveness also being somewhat subdued over the previous months, a sudden call to arms at a time when his tackle is ill-prepared, a situation below might be played out:

"Which way do you want me to come at you?" He said.

"How you normally do it. Missionary!" She spoke.

"But all I can see is your belly and not your front garden."

"Okay, what about if I stick my arse in the air?" was her solution.

Man thinks this is not going well but tries to persevere for the team!

This synopsis of pre-parenting so far highlights the common acceptance that life changes when you have a baby. Wrong. Life actually changes at the point when one plans for a family. Hitherto, the genres have completely different emotional perspectives as well as ways of dealing with conflicts and approaches. When the child is born, there is a tangible bundle of focus. Prior to that, there is conjecture, a notion of what has to be considered, where to seek advice, what you should or should not do, how you support each other, and what is important to each person in the planning and commitment stage.

Chapter 4
'What I Need Is Your Support'

The traditional male counterpart has difficulty understanding what support is actually required. His interpretation is influenced by Martian values, which is to search for a practical application to derive a perfect solution. He would be happy with the knowledge of delivering assistance in this way. He quickly realises that you cannot streamline emotional support. Such a situation may, of course, be unlikely with same-sex couples where one assumes they would exhibit a more aligned state of empathy.

Let's start with the situation where the pregnancy has become well advanced and a Martian is taking the supporting role. The mum has a chronic back ache which can occur quite often. Yep, we can do that, the man thinks, as he is more than capable of delivering the correct pressure once he knows where the area of pain has been identified. There are, however, two matters that can be a curve ball in such a situation.

Firstly, it's the question as to when the services are anticipated. If at the end of a working day, some sport is on the telly that the male would love to watch a call of duty, then becomes inconvenient. Martians would much prefer to assist when it is convenient to them rather than at the point when requested. What's more, they can become convinced that the mums-to-be purposefully choose the worst time to put in a back rub chit, i.e., either at the point of maximum tiredness or being preoccupied having settled down to the potentially most exciting sports game of the century.

"Oh, darling, my back is so sore from carrying your child. I could really do with one of your special rubs," she says.

"Can it wait? It's the European Cup with my team, Queens Park Rangers. They have never reached the final before and is not likely to happen ever again."

"But you promised when we agreed to have a baby you would always be there for me and assist when I really need your help. I do now," she responded.

"Can you just sit in one position and wait for me, which will be around forty-five minutes until the second half has finished, or possibly a bit longer if extra time or penalties is called for?"

Of course, Martians do still concede, as there is no defence when they are reminded of the joy of trying to conceive. He, however, would remain stoic in his attempt to watch the game by introducing a practical caveat that, when crumbling to the provision of the therapy, it would have to be carried out on the floor so one's eye can be kept trained on the TV.

This situation often leads to an inadequate or at best a far from acceptable manipulation of the areas requiring pain relief. Man thinks he has still complied with the plea, but the judgement from the mum is self-evident. There are no words exchanged as superfluous in such a moment. Just a raising of the eyebrow by the mum confirms there has been an abject failure in the task.

Such a situation rarely occurs where same-sex birth partners are expecting a baby. Either a Martian or Venetian couple. There is likely to be a deeper connection aligned to a similar emotional horizon one rarely achieves from interplanetary relationships, which have different value doctrines. Obviously, it is only the Venetian couple that will have a physical birth partner, and their conversation in a similar scenario could be something like this:

"Oh, darling, I have terrible back ache. Can you help me?" The birth mum asks.

"Oh, no problem. I will stop cooking and come right over to relieve your pain right away," Mum number two says.

30 minutes later:

"I smell something burning. Did you remember to turn off the oven in your haste to help me?" Birth Mum retorts.

Beep! Beep! Beep! Went the fire alarm.

"Oh, bugger," Mum number two says.

This demonstrates it is not always the best strategy to forget all else in trying to jump immediately to please the birth mum.

There is a second matter. Temptation. That is, if a back rub is requested just before lights out. Imagine a common theme. Teeth cleaned, covers turned back, and mum-to-be is half naked on her front, calling for pain-relieving back therapy with specific locations where pressure points are required.

It all starts off fairly innocuous with the only real intention of trying to make amends as to the half-hearted effort given in front of the TV in which man knows only too well that he was well and truly caught out.

"Is this the point where it hurts, dear? Am I using the right pressure to relieve your pain?" He whispers.

Mum-to-be does not really respond with more than a 'Mmm' with her face pressed firmly into the mattress. Mars man then starts to focus on her aurora and tenderness of the skin and makes the cardinal sin to suggest that perhaps baby oil would assist. With her mouth still muffled into the sheets, another, but longer "Mmmmmmm." This is taken as confirmation as to what a good idea the oil would be. The soft and slippery lotion is loaded into the hand. Much care is taken to warm the oil to match the back temperature prior to application. The hands are cupped before sensually spreading onto the strained area from carrying the baby. It's not long until the workman-like effort turns into potential foreplay as the handling becomes ever more sensual, heading way down the back, past the buttocks, and still further.

There is now a hope in the mind of the male masseuse that something more may be in the offing, reflected by a stretchiness in Mars man's underpants. He thinks *my god, a moment made from dreams*. A few seconds pass where no words are said. He prays to heaven for the all-clear to attempt a home score but is soon quelled by a knockout blow from the muffled mouth still buried in the sheet.

"Really," she drawls disapprovingly.

This situation demonstrates where the thought processes of the two sexes deviate and call for understanding. The woman would be thinking, how can an innocuous and specifically requested massage due to a painful back from carrying the baby be construed as foreplay? Whereas he would consider it wasn't pre-mediated but spawned out of being connected to the Venetian's aura and not his fault.

Indeed, it should be viewed as a compliment. I delivered the massage as requested, so she should be really grateful for my attentiveness.

Shopping. No further introduction is needed to this matter. Let's assess pre- and post-pregnancy habits and attitudes. Before a family is considered by the couple, Venetians like to shop, shop and shop. There may not be anything specific on the list, but just a general 'mooch' is the order of the day. Perhaps being too disingenuous in that they may have an idea of something that is needed but remains a non-specific item. Thus, a trip to the madness of a retail shopping centre on a Saturday afternoon is still justified. It would just be too awful to wait when an actual purchase is needed.

A common Martian view is avoiding the shopping centre stampede to when it is absolutely necessary. He never goes just to graze on a whim. There requires not only a very specific item needed but where the importance of the purchase cannot be delayed any further. He may be forced to go into a town centre on occasion by his Venetian where an item of clothing has so worn out or seriously out of fashion that he is in danger of being subject to that constant looking up and down of his attire combined with 'Are you seriously thinking of wearing that!' He wouldn't, however, have any problem spending time in the hardware store selecting even the smallest of items or weighing up paint products as to whether a monetary saving warrants a risk in quality, but there is no danger of a spontaneous trip where clothes are concerned. The focus being an attempt to schedule the now enforced shopping trip demanded by his Venetian to coincide with any promotion time to save a few pennies.

The Martian does not need to get involved in the habitual trip to the high street of his Venetian during this time. He may get asked on occasion, but an excuse of needing to finish that DIY project or gardening, albeit he may just be lounging appreciating the time in his home alone is accepted. There is no Spanish Inquisition as to what really is so important for the non-accompaniment. This all changes when the baby is on the way.

Martians do not really baulk at doing the odd trip to get what a baby may need. Particularly if this involves a flat pack item of furniture where he knows he can complete its assembly, obtaining (in his mind) a raft of brownie points as a job well done. But every weekend! The Venetian behaviour built up over the years that when an item is thought about, its purchase needs to be instant now comes into conflict with the Martian's concept of shopping. The Martian is aware he needs to show willingness, but showing support without a sulk or a long face as you drive down to the five thousand space parking area is hard to hide. Man does this in a number of ways, contemplating in his thoughts rational possibilities to side-step from having to be constantly in attendance. When can I claim the first coffee? Is it possible to suggest to your Venetian, "I will sit in the cafe and give you time to look around without me so I don't distract you from what you want to buy?" Can you limit the time somehow by saying you need to return home by a certain time? All Martians know is that they are on pretty weak ground to suggest anything that is a hint of not giving the experience your full support. All these thoughts are quickly forgotten even before the barrier lifts into the plaza.

"As I am now pregnant, could you find a parking space near the front door of the mall?" She enquiringly says.

The man thinks but dares not say that pregnancy is not a disease and has no impact on the ability to put one foot in front of the other. Indeed, in a few minutes, you will have absolutely no problem covering a distance of a few miles up and down the concourse of the shops. Instead, "Okay, I will do my best."

After a few minutes of going around and around, there are no other spaces within two hundred metres of the entrance, creating a potentially explosive situation when you pass row and row of empty bays immediately in front with the yellow markings indicating 'For the sole use of the disabled or mother and child'.

"Why don't you park there? I have a child. It just happens to be in my belly. Look, I am just as disabled as that person who just got out of their car, so I must have every right to park in this area. Don't you agree?" She states.

Oh boy. It is arguably the most stressful moment in a domestic situation sharing your life with a Venetian. You know her logic is completely wrong, but you want to be supportive. On the other hand, you do not want to be that person who has to explain to the parking attendant when he points out your blindness or intelligence of not seeing or reading the very clear signage of the priority for parking standing aloft in front of your bay. So, what would happen? Move to another parking area further away or remain and stand your ground with the potential of receiving a penalty notice. Absolutely no idea.

The concept of how the Martian 'giveth' support and the Venetian 'receiveth' is a constantly recurring situation. The

Martian does not attempt to assist in a way that is purposefully antagonistic or inappropriate. It's just because their planetary rules or skills do not match those from Venus, where the empathy conflicts with his view of the world or cannot be solved by a more practical intervention.

Chapter 5
'Naming Baby'

When is the right time to choose a name? The majority of men would not consider the baby's title as a high priority. That is to say, leave until the very last minute. The thought process is that he would rather not have the endless debates that will inevitably occur, preferring to adopt a more intuitive approach as labour happens. Just miss out on the middle man, please, as we fear that as the baby is born, we are almost certainly to hear the words.

"Oh, doesn't he/she look like an X? I know we decided on Y/Z (well the Venetian did) but he does rather look like X. Do you agree, babe?" She enquires.

The male response would be a 'Yes, darling' cursing under his breath, saying what the f...k were the last few months about utilising every method and historical connections to select the name.

Considering how Venetians attend to such matters, there is a game of naming tennis to play. Men would just concede the match at the start and not get drawn into a grand slam tournament where there is no natural end to the fifth set. The final winning stroke is only determined by the Venetian when she decides sufficient debating time has been allocated.

The first task is to consider where inspiration should be drawn from. Does this process have to include a name for both boy and girl if the sex of the baby is unknown? An even more daunting proposition is if an alpha Venetian is involved. Imagine the forensic testing of the chosen names, which more than likely would lead to the setting up of a specific selection panel. Not just parents, grandparents and close friends, but pulling people off the street as they walk past the front door. Would the alpha also consider this a further call for a flip chart, a voting matrix, and a full description under each category of the names, including their historic origins? Of course, and for the unfortunate partner, the head falls into his hands just thinking about what may be in store.

Baby naming books (albeit very twentieth century) were some of the most cherished publications in the birth library of some Venetians. One book ought to be sufficient, possibly two, as the smart publishers provide separate girl- and boy-naming compendiums. Never. Even non-alpha Venetians consider cross-referencing to more than one source. A situation now not dissimilar to choosing a comparison site for the purchase of insurance. The child-naming tennis match was about to begin.

"What about this name and this or this? Forget all that, oh, I do like this one," she would say.

And on it goes for what always feels like an hour or three by the male.

No conclusion is ever reached in the first stab at a suitable child label. To the surprise of men, this is one occasion where Venetians could adopt a more systematic approach. Five books, five pieces of paper. The matrix methodology would naturally end up with a very long list. To whittle down those considered potentially suitable may involve how each in turn would sound for a lifetime of use. Each could choose their own contributions, but even at this stage, the male would realise any idea of his would (somewhere along the process) get discarded. This only causes his energy level to dip even further whilst turning into a cynic.

"What about George Ringo Paul John or Horatio on the boys' list and Nelly or Rapunzel for a girl?" He would suggest.

"You either take this seriously or I will just pick the names without you," she responds.

This was of course exactly what he wanted to hear, but before he stated, "Oh yes. Please, you just choose," he remembered the lessons he had learnt and that such a situation required more than just a benign "Okay." Instead, with a sheepish and guilty look as to his misdemeanour, "Okay, I will up my game and try and think of proper names you might consider as being a worthy contribution. Huh, I was only joking, dear. Of course, I am just as interested as you in the name."

Persevering with this set, back and forth, long into the night, a final 'short' list of twenty per gender was agreed. It was now time for a sifting and shake-out. Do any of these suggestions have a horrid connotation? For example, a son named Vlad could be known as 'Vlad the Impaler' or a choice of Damian people may subtly bully that child by singing a score from the Omen films (or latterly the comedy 'Only Fools and Horses'). For a girl named Matilda, this could set the image of our girl having creepy button eyes, imitating the character in the borderline children's movie.

What about cutting or moving up those names with a historical context that may offend or delight? Archils would be an unlikely candidate, but Jason as of the Argonauts could have been a good thought. Indeed, Marc Anthony or Joan (as of Joan of Arc fame). A Martian suggesting such contenders would be viewed as not taking the matter seriously…and Venetians would be right!

The hottest topic would be reserved for known names of family and friends. Not only names in existence but those that may occur in the future. A Venetian would test for every angle and situation, including how the initials would work. Teresa would not be suited with a surname of Green. Such a poor coupling was demonstrated by all the old 'Carry on…' comedy films of the 1960s and 1970s. They were funny such a Sid Plummer being the Foreman at the toilet factory owned by WC Boggs. *Carry on Cowboy* starred Marshal P Knutt and included a Native American Chief Big Heap. In our family, it was the letter 'S' that was troublesome and had to be navigated away from. Between the relatives, there had been so many divorces that there were six female Christian names that had the same prefix with only two actual in-laws and the majority were classed as out-laws.

The second issue was whether, through conversations in the mother groups, someone else already had the same name on their list. Bearing in mind it was still a list, and as we know, there is no telling what the final selection would be going forward. This is a stage where the naming progress remained in the quagmire of indecision as the game was heading to the third set.

Whilst the mix of contributors required would invariably be drawn by the intending parents from both planets, we now know (or can guess) how this set would be played out. Those other women from Venus involved would completely engage in the process. On hearing the news that there would be a specific evening drinks session set aside for this task of baby naming, the excitement becomes immense, or at least it does for the Venetians. The Martian counterparts, of course, would try to maintain a low bar of discussion, limiting responses to cursory nods of the head at the right moment just to reaffirm. (In particular, those who had already been through the trauma of such a grand slam tournament match for their infants.)

Set four was all about searching for any endorsement for the slightly shorter list of now ten suggestions for each genre. Any situation that could be found by the Venetian mother-to-be to have a naming-the-baby conversation was subconsciously planned. The groceries trip, the midwife's check-up, the bus queue. No situation would escape. Not that this process assists in narrowing down the field as to the eventual name.

The final set of five had arrived. Time spent at this stage has already included initial thoughts, amendments, new entries, and those struck off to attain a top three for a baby boy or girl. Off we go:

"We have three names for each sex. You must now tell me your favourite," she says. "Which name would you prefer?"

"I am happy to go with your selection," Mars man bats back.

"Please, darling. I want to hear your choice, as this is a joint decision." He thinks, really!

"Okay then. I like X."

"Why do you like that one?" She enquires.

A Martian's attempt to concede the match of the name choice using a repetition of the phrase, 'I just do' struggles to convince the Venetians this set has been played in the best of spirits. Searching for credible reasons when whatever is offered is likely to be a waste of good oxygen. The moment becomes stressful but essential for continued harmony. As such a strategy played out on Mars becomes highly valuable. This is the concept of offering up a sacrificial suggestion. As anticipated, the suitability of this name was shot down in flames, which was great news and greeted with a warm sensation of delight that some of the old skills learnt on our planet still have a degree of relevance on Earth.

Such a five-set tie would generally last between the prospective parents to the day of the birth. Revisit after revisit as to the justification for the mum's choice. In this situation and for the greater good, we Martians carry on unabated to return the serve, ground strokes, and lobs until the match-winning shot was struck for the final name.

One final twist is with a prayer and a hope that the baby that arrives suits the choice. If not, it's back to a further round of discussion.

Nearly all Martians having been through this process come to the conclusion that as long as my Venetian is happy, then I shall be more than delighted to register, after the birth, her chosen name. Including first, second or third. And in the exact same order. Well, you would think so, wouldn't you? But not in my case, and this is actually true.

My Venetian mum decided on a theme. From what was told, it's a little incredulous that the thrust was to use a well-known name from each of the four United Kingdom countries. Mine was Ivor and clearly very Welsh. It did not go through the sifting rules. The first rule was broken. Odd connotations and how the name could be used in jest were also not considered. The first that springs to mind is Ivan the Terrible. Nice. Latterly, considering what else my name could be tied to, was the story about the good knight Ivanhoe which was altogether more pleasing. But the most major misdemeanour was not being tuned in…literally to the story writer and teller Oliver Postgate. His Welsh dragon and engine children's story 'Ivor the Engine' became legendary. Not only the book would have been a clue but before being born, they had already produced a black-and-white children's cartoon. Thus, a lifetime was to be had with kids and colleagues spouting in my face in a very poor version of a Welsh accent 'Ivor the Engine'. I don't, however, blame her for not predicting that my first job was to be an engineer but any attempt to get my goat with name calling was so easy and just needed to roll off the tongue, 'Ivor the Engineeeeeeeer'.

The realisation of my parent's choice that clearly had not been adequately screened did not end there. Let's break the name down. Ivor can become comparable to 'I have a'. So 'Ivor question for you' or 'Ivor (I have) a lot' but the most excruciating reference was 'Ivor big one'. If only. But the extraordinary reaction was when such references were contained within birthday and Christmas cards such as 'Have a great one big' un'. Of course, Mum would just say, 'That's nice, dear' not realising the path she had set.

Having chosen the first name, it looks as though the consultation went wider so as to include at least the grandparents. The tradition for the second Christian name 'John' had already been taken by my elder brother. As such, the two other contenders were an English 'James' and a multilingual 'Robert'. The chain-smoking Nan was clearly on the Venetian panel; the mum of my father. Being a staunch traditionalist, she thought the name choice of Ivor was abhorrent. Knowing the two personalities, one could imagine this exchange could have followed:

"Why would you want a boy's name like Ivor?" Nan could have said with no scruples.

"We (The royal we) have decided on the theme to choose names relating to home nations, and the one for Wales has been chosen as Ivor," Mum said.

"Well, I don't like it. What's wrong with the traditional names in our family, such as Robert?"

The will of Nan communicated by a steadfast glare to my father that she expected nothing less than to stand with her staunch view culminated in an olive branch to be handed out.

"Mum. It is not my intention to upset or exclude you so we can add Robert as a second name," Dad interjected.

"Can't it be the first name instead?" She retorted.

"No. It cannot. We have ourselves decided it will be Ivor." Sternly stated by my mother-to-be.

One would have thought this was the end of the matter, but come the day of registration, Dad either had an aberration or indeed was terrified of defying his mother. Probably the latter, as he was to come up with a cunning plan to somehow register the name in the order demanded by his mum. Robert Ivor James.

It is unfathomable how this Martian thought he could get away with changing the express wishes of a Venetian when he knows at some point he is going to present the birth certificate in all its glory. Did he think the switching of the name order would be the end of the matter? Yes. Was there a ready excuse as to why he misunderstood? Also, an emphatic yes.

"I was so confused at the consultation panel that I thought we had finally concluded the name of Robert would be the first, being in agreement with my mum."

All that is known was that a baptism was arranged six weeks later. I had acquired a second certificate re-instigating the first name to Ivor. The lesson here for Martians is that there would be no stone left unturned for a Venetian who believes any decision made together is one that cannot be undone unless it is signed in blood. His blood. There is a second lesson for any men out there wanting to follow a path of deceit influenced by their mum. Just think of the child. Can you imagine the confusion for the rest of his life that would be caused by having two different name orders on separate birth certificates? You can't. Well, that would be another story.

Chapter 6
Let's Prepare the Birthing Bag

One of the delights for many a Venetian is packing a bag. Any bag but specifically the birthing bag. Given a situation where there are objects to be transported for a special occasion, the pleasure is somewhat exponentially increased. It is not just a question of what to put in the selected holdall but to do so at the earliest opportunity. For Martians, packing clothes is a wholesome chore and a task to be actioned as quickly as possible. Usually, at the eleventh hour and fifty-ninth minute.

When is the right time? Too early, and you might forget what has been neatly folded and meticulously ordered in the case. Does one delay so as not to make a judgement call until all the latest birthing information is known? On the other hand, too late and the essential refining period may be insufficient to get every last item in the bag one could possibly need.

Advice is therefore sought but does not involve Martians. As my Nan used to say, their knowledge as to when and what is required is about as useful as a chocolate tea pot. It's a question first aimed at the midwife. Although an infamous list has to be prepared, it does not curtail the endless round of discussions with the partner, although he has strictly no involvement. In this example, the following list has been assumed:

For her hospital stay	For baby
2 night dresses	*New born nappies*
1 Robe	*Baby grows*
3 pairs of knickers	*vest*
1 pair of slippers	*Boy/girl attire (if sex is known)*
Toiletries	*Blanket*
1 Towel	*hat*

In my mother's time, if birth was not considered to have any foreseeable complications, it was quite okay to deliver at home. Mums would have their mums at the ready to do all the pampering and care for as long as necessary after the birth. This also saved any requirement to pack the 'birthing bag' as all the clothes and paraphernalia would be already on hand. If a hospital birth was deemed necessary, then it could be as long as ten days. Oh, imagine the packing required for this length of time.

Being born at my Nan's home in North London, I describe a true but stereotypical event for the era between males and females regarding attitudes to child birth. Yes, a point in time has not dawned on both sexes that we talk, feel and react differently for certain situations and not yet discovered why our interplanetary communication can potentially appear out of cinque.

The front room was laid out for the purpose of my birth. In the mid-twentieth century, home owners had a strange practice where the front room, often the largest in the house, was used to entertain guests or only for Sunday best. When staying there for a few days, even in the 1960s, we would never go into the 'front room' to play. It was not an outright ban but an unsaid rule. My mother took residence a few days before the birth date 'in the front room' as a more practical solution than her small tenement flat in Archway, North London. There was also a desire to have on hand the family doctor. At this time, Mum's brother was still in residence. He worked for the GPO (Now British Telecom) and was out for most of the day dealing with the network.

It was a morning in mid-April when kick-off occurred. The first contractions were felt and continued throughout the day. By late afternoon, my history was about to commence, readying myself to come into this world. It was also about the time mum's brother returned home and thought nothing of his sister giving birth to me in the 'front room'. To him, it was just the normal end of the day when he would slip off his shoes at the entrance by the door and Nan would get his supper ready.

It should have been obvious, but not to him, that she was not in the kitchen preparing the meal but with his sister. Surely there was a clue from the periodic howling as the contractions continued to tighten.

By now, it was 5:45 pm, and tea was late by a wholly unacceptable fifteen minutes. This disturbance to a Martian routine is both very perplexing and confusing as to what action should be taken. Hunger pains need to be quelled, and yet something else has taken priority.

"Mum, Mum, are you in there?" (In the front room). He said.

"Yes, dear," she replied.

"My tea is late, and I am hungry. How long?" He continued.

"Can't you hear your sister is giving birth? You just have to wait!" She said in a stern and frustrated tone.

It was not long before I came into this world. Ultimately, Uncle did not have to wait that long for his tea, but to him it was a lifetime. Imagine a returning young adult being a fellow Venetian. The response would certainly be somewhat more empathetic.

"Oh, my sis. Is there anything I can do to help? Don't worry about me, Mum, I can get something to eat myself."

It was not that my uncle was uncaring. Indeed, we had latterly a pretty close relationship. It's just at that moment in time that our priorities are deflected due to a Martian focus on maintaining a routine. His routine.

This type of scenario rarely happens today, so back to the story as to the 'birthing bag'. First and foremost, the type. For Martians, the bag should be no drama. Just sufficient to fit all that had been specified, which would likely be any old holdall. The choice of birthing bag for men. Certainly not a suitcase, and definitely forget a pull-along Samsonite long hall flight bag, as this would be somewhat embarrassing traipsing such a humongous number of accessories for a short two-day stay around the hospital. Men would think the clue is in the name. 'A birthing bag'. A strut into the hospital with the holdall swung on to the back with a nonchalant swagger would be far, far cooler.

Putting the bag choice to one side, we have the defined list. Unfortunately, most women only see the items as headings and a starter for ten. Night dresses. Are these to be long or short? Is there a requirement to button up half way or the full-length type? Better to take all the variations. Should this and all items be name-tagged to identify who they belong to in case there is an epidemic of births on the day (or night!)? There is a feeling of uncertainty as each 'heading' is run through in turn and a subject to be returned to time and time again with the midwife and within the soon-to-be-formed parent's group.

It quickly becomes obvious there is no right or wrong in what you need to take. Just preferences. As we have learnt, this does not halt a full-on debate for all items, as this helps a Venetian to decide but where a Martian could be called on to carry out a sense check (in the loosest of terms!).

"Don't you think one of those will do?"

"Do you really need a backup toothbrush?"

"Yes, I have packed your hairdryer and curling tongues, but is the roller set really necessary?"

Then it is the debate for specific 'toiletries'. Would a spray deodorant be acceptable or does it have to be a roll-on? Can I use an electric toothbrush? Thank goodness, he would think at least there has been no suggestion to include Martian equipment due to his attendance at the future birth, perhaps for a morning shave.

Moving on to the new born clothes is the added dilemma as to gender. If unknown, what do you do? Go for multi-purpose outfits or take a boys and girls jumper, trousers and a dress. In the past, the choice was easy. Just stick them in a white frock that is double the size of the baby. Times have changed with a focus that gender identification may be preferred. Possibly a worry that if the new born has the typical baldness, a blue or pink outfit could at least identify the sex. It can take away the embarrassment for all concerned when great gran comes along and says, "Who is a pretty boy then?" when actually the newest of family members is a baby girl.

The midwife's list is now put to one side for the mums to prepare their own personal versions. This takes the form of a number of drafts. First pencilled so that changes can be erased. Second, the items are over written with an ink pen once draft ten has been created. This stage would have been the final version to be scrutinised with anyone prepared to listen and engage, except of course our men, who just nod with an occasional 'that sounds fine'. Possibly, this schedule is created on an iPad, smartphone notes, or a laptop computer, but a physical list remains relevant. With all that effort to prepare, there isn't anything like ticking off each item as it is placed carefully in the birthing bag.

The matter of when the bag has been prepared is not the only consideration. Where do you place the suitcase or holdall in the home so it becomes readily available when the time has come to trot off to the maternity ward? Martians would stick the chosen carrier in some cupboard somewhere with the full knowledge that they know where it is located. Venetians have a tendency to overthink as to a particular potential set of circumstances. This can lead to the fear of a very unlikely prospect that by lodging the birthing bag in the said cupboard it could be forgotten. Nah, surly not possible.

The Venetian's decision is that the birthing bag now has to take pride of place by the front door. It does not matter that every time you walk over the threshold, the now bulging bag falls over and trips you up. By now, the bag that has been packed very early has a covering of dust on the top, becoming a health hazard.

In reality, all this pales into insignificance, reflecting a tiny chink in the process; that of the male is supposed to bring the bag with him to the maternity ward.

"We need to go now. The contractions have started. F**K me, they're painful. Why did you agree to start a family?" She said.

"Right, O, I will get the car ready for you, darling. Don't worry, we will soon be at the hospital."

The car motor starts to hum, and the door flung open for his wife. (Which he hasn't done for a very long time since he was trying to impress how romantic he could be.) He then returns to the front door and grabs his wife by the arm, closing the house entrance as he leads her down the drive.

"Let's go. I have opened the door for you, so as soon as you swing round on the seat we can get to the hospital in good time," he says.

Five minutes into the journey:

"Where's the f***king birthing bag?"

Although the suitcase is by the front door, it still does not stop a Martian in his singular project of getting his wife to the maternity unit from forgetting he has another responsibility. He doesn't think it's such a big deal as at some point he will be able to return and collect. In his thought process driving towards the hospital, he would be surprised if there wasn't a lost property box or a collection of hand-me-down baby clothes on the ward available in the short term but realises it is not a thought to be shared. For the time being, it's a matter of a sorry grovel. One wouldn't want to raise the stress levels before we even get through the door of the labour ward for the next stage of the birthing experience.

Chapter 7
Monitoring Through Pregnancy

Part of the excitement or chore of making sure all is well with the unborn child very much depends on what planet you come from. Those from Venus ensure the regular trips to the hospital or anti-natal classes are both fully diarised through the pregnancy and are awaited with wholesome anticipation. For Martians, it is a different kettle of fish. How to hide the boredom whilst being supportive as having to put aside time they hope does not clash with something far more important such as work?

There is, however, one exception to this general rule. It is the first scan where Martians will have a huge pride to see what he has achieved during the conception stage. There remains an inability to show openly any form of exaltation, especially in front of the radiographer.

The news of the date for the first scan contained within an envelope from the hospital flops through the box and hits the mat. The confirmed appointment is met with a little jig around the room from the mum. The dad just raises an eyebrow from his prostrate position stretched out on the sofa with an indignation as to what did you expect as the arrival of this letter was fully advised by the doctor.

The normal wait for any hospital appointment becomes excruciatingly painful for both. Mum as she rehearses the infinite scenarios as to what will be seen. Both have the same thought. First and foremost, as to whether the unborn child has all the right pieces in the right places. The mum focuses on whether you will be able to see if they resemble anybody in the family. The dad's mind strays to if the baby is a boy. How does its 'tackle' look? Not necessarily the length, as even to the most undiscerning male one assumes it would bear no relation to the final size but whether you can see two well-formed cherries on either side of the cocktail stick.

The day arrives. It necessitates a thirty-minute car journey. It is unusually quiet in the vehicle. No chat. Even no bickering as to which distinguishingly planetary intelligence has a better sense of direction. All that can be heard is the low background tone from the radio, as both are deep within their own subconscious, mulling over their personal expectations as to what will shortly be the moment when it is their turn to sense the enormity of what they have both created.

Even the selection of where to park and how close to the entrance one can fit the car into a marked bay passes without comment. Not quite the stress as occurred on the weekly; let's see what we also need trips to the shopping centre. The only exchange of normality is limited to the outrageous parking charge for the privilege of the hospital visit, which should be free and part of the taxes we pay. Of course, a topic choice of the Martian. The location of the maternity wing and the tortuous route through the corridors do, however, become the navigation topic of the day.

"I can't possibly remember how to get there when I am just about to give birth," she said.

"It's not that hard," he says in a condescending voice. He sees the error of what he has just said and follows up with, "I will be with you all the way, my darling."

She was thinking, what if he is not with me and it is in the middle of the night? He was thinking. Where's the drama? It's a bleeding hospital with someone around all the time. What would she like me to do? Come beforehand and drop a trail of gingerbread.

In the waiting room, the previous parents-to-be walked past and out of the scan room. They were grinning like Cheshire cats, clutching a small piece of paper pointing furiously at the black-and-white etching as if it were a masterpiece. Nah, we are more composed. That would never be us. It's our turn now.

"Would you come this way? Lie on the bench and roll up your top," the radiographer said.

The air was filled with a touch of nervousness as thoughts turned to the ultimate reason that such an examination was essential at this time in the pregnancy. Is the foetus all good? In a few moments that would be known.

Just before, there was a small shrill contained within a large gasp of breath as the cold ultrasound receiver met with the sea of jelly on her now bloated stomach. And there it was. Our baby viewed for the first time.

The experience was a lot different thirty-odd years ago when the resolution on the screen was such that it was hard to see through all the black-and-white shadowing whether you could see a new life form or was it really a photograph of a tadpole just handed out to give comfort to the parents.

It was also tougher to ascertain the sex of the baby and certainly always unlikely to be able to fully count that all the digits were there and correct. One could barely distinguish if there was a dangly bit and was a skill best left to the experts.

"Look there, I can see his willy. That's fantastic. It's a boy!" said the man.

"No, that's the chord attached to the placenta!" replied the radiographer.

Nowadays, it is a lot easier to see what you are supposed to be looking at, even without such guidance from the nursing staff in attendance. Certainly, one can only absolutely confirm if it's a boy from full-frontal exposure. If the little cherub decides to position itself with the backside up, it must be impossible. There is generally a later opportunity for a further scan regarding the great reveal. If the baby continues to be obstinate or parents do not wish to know the gender, then the birthing bag packing will continue to take on the uncertainty of what to include.

To continue with a semblance of mystic couples may not wish to know the sex even if it could be distinguished. The Mars chap would have however applied his logic at the moment the question is posed by the radiographer. If she asks whether one wants to know the gender, one can assume that it must be a boy. De facto, being able to see the 'thingy'. So, be advised. If you want to keep the sex of your baby secret, then tell the attendant before you enter the room that you do not want to know.

The Martian's reaction to this event is untypical. The emotion, which includes a mix of relief that all is well and the sublime joy of seeing a new life, is very foreign to him. It does not square with the emotional order Mars man likes to consider as their self: viz., practical and in control. It becomes one of those moments where a large intake of breath has to be taken to hide the feelings of grace and tenderness as to what has just occurred. Subconsciously, he can now partially understand the emotional gig Venetians are always on about when such moments occur on their planet.

True to type kicks back in for the ante-natal classes. Most men know the importance of being the archetypical supportive birth partner and showing a willingness to attend every class they can. He starts off with all good intentions but knows he has to put to one side his tendency to feel a tinge of embarrassment in becoming a dad in front of others. He baulks at the notion there are at least six of such classes and hopes that most will be in the afternoon so the ace card of an important and unavoidable work situation can be proffered as a legitimate excuse not to attend all such sessions. It is fairly clear that if these classes were one-on-one with the community worker or a midwife, it would not be so daunting compared with the abject fear that comes with a group of new parents and containing fellow men.

When walking into the first ante-natal class, Venetians are excited by the prospect of mixing with others from the same planet. The exchange of their story and the magic of being pregnant is told in fine detail to whoever wishes to listen. That normally includes the whole class. Whereas men focus on how little information can be exchanged and to a quantum they can get away with, at the same time ensuring their partners do not judge that the lack of dialogue could be translated as being disinterested in the process.

After the pre-chats are completed, participants are called to take a place in the dreaded circle of seats. This situation is not uncommon for women, as it's a natural phenomenon where the roots can be traced back to the seventies disco and the dancing around a clutch of handbags in the centre of the floor (where men preferred swaying with a pint of liquid refreshment in the one hand, trying not to spill a drop!). Men take a guarded approach as to what they believe is about to potentially come their way. Open questions requiring responses to be vocalised to all. Men can manage to spout their names in a forum, but where slightly personal details are necessary, there is a clear stutter or an uncomfortable hesitancy. An exception to this is a technique learnt on Mars. Try and make a joke or speak with some sarcasm when answering.

"Tell us about your story," the leader asked.

"What, how did my wife end up pregnant? Haha!"

With this approach, it was now unlikely that another question would be directed at them. It was safe to now lean back in the seat with some confidence of making it to the end of the session without a further forum contribution.

Once the Q&A session had ended, the competitiveness of who could master the exercises or the breathing techniques being best in class commenced. To women, it's about the attentiveness and participation of their partner. To men, it's about not making a fool out of yourself, or at least, not being as big a tit as the other future dads.

This situation did not entirely relate to yours truly having already had the basic knowledge from childhood. No, I was not responsible for a teen baby but became involved by default. Mum, when moving to the small and growing town of Royston, noticed that there were no ante-natal facilities. This was a situation that was abhorrent to her, and she decided after her third child she would volunteer and seek training from the National Childbirth Trust. Once proficient, the setting up of a local group was feasible, and that is what she did.

Not recalling the specifics of the training Mum had, but for a child looking on, in the same house, there seemed to be odd adult behaviour going on. Particularly when explanations were proffered in a rudimentary way as to how childbirth works.

Yes, the infamous circle was formed. Not all matching chairs but a collection of comfy high back front room types, dining chairs, and an old stool from the kitchen. The group invariably numbered six to eight women. Note, no men. It was not because the session was held in the afternoon as definitely early evening, but the participation of males was not encouraged or deemed necessary. (A very pleasing situation for a number of men happy to stay on the touchline.) The roll call could be distinctly heard by us children, although we were barred from the front room to the upstairs. Curiosity hung in the air as to what was going to happen.

At the first meeting, Mum, like a magician, presented an old pink shoe box. It was adapted where a piece of yellow chair-filling foam had replaced the rectangular base. It looked as if it were a couple of centimetres thick with a slit in the middle for about half its length. The baby-like doll was placed in the box with the lid firmly shut. Taking the magician theme to the next step, it was like pulling a rabbit out of a hat as her hand fed into the spongy slit and, hey presto, out popped the doll's head first. At the age of six, the full explanation as to giving birth was not proffered, but for a short while, my assumption was babies came from a Clarks company shoebox and not via a stork! For the mothers, I am sure they got the gist from mum's Janet & John approach (a series of children's books from the sixties to help children read and explain the world in the simplest of ways) as to what would happen. The only amateur dramatic demonstration that appeared to be missing being pulled out of the shoe box was something from the fridge, such as an offal to simulate the afterbirth.

As time progressed in the sessions, there were similar floor exercises akin to the modern class in a community hall or health centre. In our house, this required the use of foam pillows for the pregnant ladies' comfort that had been collated. Knowing Mum, she would have begged for a free contribution from any upholstery shop. These were all shapes and sizes. The pulling out of a cupboard for the session became part of our weekly household rough playtime. One of the three would stand up at the top of the stairs and throw the cushions down one by one towards and at the others standing at the bottom. This was to the sound of raucous laughter and much to my mum's annoyance. On the odd occasion, the 'thrower' forgot to let go and rolled down with the same momentum as the foam step by step. No tears, but with a stiff upper lip, I would get up with a rub of the body part that had contact with the edge of the riser, the bannister, or the side of the wall.

It was a godsend that the birthing ball had not been invented and no thought of using a 'Space Hopper' (a bouncing ball toy) as a substitute. Although arguably this spherical orb would have performed better having two rubbery udders for the hands to grab for those less agile of mums in the class. Just imagine if one was included with the various foam articles that were present in our home. A mere tumble as the ball was rolled down the stairs would quickly turn into an Apollo-type space launch through the front door.

The following episode did not happen but demonstrates the problem with home teaching while the domestic activities continue. Imagine all the pregnant ladies lying prostrate on the floor waiting for the instruction to breathe. "In…hold…and breathe out." She had a particular way of answering the phone, which she never changed. "Hello. Sylvia here. Pause as the caller gave their name. Oh, hello." With such a phone interruption and a lengthy conversation, the vision is one of the ladies being told to breathe in but with no instruction to exhale. The resultant situation is that all their faces turn blue!

Throughout the pregnancy, the worry that all is well is a never-ending haze in the background. It is difficult for Martians to know when there is an inevitable moment of fear that all is not well, which warrants a trip to the hospital. The working assumption is that childbirth is the most natural animal phenomenon. What could go wrong?

It's understood that the first pregnancy is a newbie situation. The body is changing and expanding. I am unsure whether the plethora of self-help avenues—either books or using the internet—is a help or hindrance. Yes, it is easy to self-diagnose, but does this allay any fears or actually hasten the rush to seek medical help? Depending on which planet you are from, you can draw completely different conclusions. It is fairly obvious that if the baby starts kicking less, one ought to seek advice sooner rather than later, but sometimes, just sometimes, it's the obvious condition and not a doomsday scenario.

"Oh, babes, I have really bad stomach pains should I go to the hospital?" She states.

"Hang on. Let me 'google it'," he says.

A quote from the search engine result via: womenshealthmag.com states.

"Trapped wind can be very uncomfortable—you may feel bloated and your stomach may make rumbling or gurgling noises, resulting in excessive 'free wind' (also known as burping or farting). Excess gas usually occurs after having eaten."

"It's just the curry I made for you tonight, so no worries," he retorts.

So as far as he is concerned, the nature of the discomfort had been researched, the reason identified, and therefore the matter closed.

This is sometimes insufficient for the mum and for the next half hour more googling is undertaken to verify the information provided, as Venetians have difficulty accepting the views of those from Mars.

Upon further investigation, the following information is revealed:

"Stomach (abdominal) pains or cramps are common in pregnancy. They're usually nothing to worry about, but they can sometimes be a sign of something more serious that needs to be checked. It's probably nothing to worry about if the pain is mild and goes away when you change position, have a rest, do a poo or pass wind."

To the Martian, the statement pretty much says the same; too much spice in the curry, but the hint of it could be something else cancels out the most obvious reason or common sense. Instead, the situation leads to the Venetian wanting to speed off to seek proper medical assistance.

After the now twenty-minute car journey and given it's late at night (notwithstanding the bonus of actually being able to park next to the hospital entrance), the waiting commences. After being booked and checked in by the first line of the medical team taking the basic personal details, it starts to become clear the wait would be a while as a non-emergency. Two hours later, the doctor on call turns up.

"Okay, can you let me feel your tummy? Mmm, I see," he says. "What have you eaten recently?"

"A home-made curry," she responds.

"I think once you have passed a number two, you will be fine."

The Martian at least learned valuable lessons from this particular dramatization. During the pregnancy, he stopped making spicy meals and was able to keep an 'I told you so' card in his back pocket for another day. A smug smile was sufficient for the journey home that he was right on this occasion.

Chapter 8
Birth Planning 'I Want a Water Birth'

As part of the new reality of childbirth, it is a Martian's view that planning to excess bears no additional fruit. There are infinite ways one could 'enjoy' the experience. These days, one can even decide to have a caesarean delivery based on a vanity choice to maintain a flat tum and intact front bum. Nature, in the end, must take its course. A question that has to be asked is whether there is a modern cultural reinvention going on to be simply different from how your parents described the process.

In the early modern era, it was pretty much a choice as decided by the midwife and doctor. There was sometimes only a cursory consultation with the mum. Either a home birth or the local maternity hospital was the order of the day. When it came to pain relief, the palette was limited.

Martians do have empathy with our partners where it becomes extremely difficult to stand by and watch their loved one in such agony. Any relief from the anguish relayed by facial physical contortions or the uncontrollable spasm resulting in a fingernail vice into our arm is very much welcomed.

At the time, when nitrous oxide, commonly labelled 'Laughing Gas' was generally the only pain relief available, one hoped this could be transported in the form of a portable tank. A vision comes to mind of a very large forty-seven kilogramme gas bottle. (The size as used for domestic LPG fuel when no mains supply exists.) Imagine having to carry such a humongous vessel up the stairs for a home birth in a block of flats. The midwife and the doctor between them with their medical bags trying to manoeuvre around corners on the return stairs is not an image or situation even the professionals would have thought they would need to consider when taking up their vocation.

Laughing Gas has of course been the butt of many a comedy film in the ninety-sixties and seventies, and sure it made more than one appearance in the suite of 'carry-on' films. These references have been very appreciated in the humorous anecdotes book for Martians when a lighter moment is needed as labour commences. I'm sure many a birth partner has said to the midwife, "Thanks for bringing me the gas; I'm going to need it."

Or:

"Can we share having one puff at a time?"

Or:

"Don't worry, love, I will be laughing with you all the way!"

This approach is now not as likely with pain relief by injection. In future, Martians would have to go in other directions to demonstrate their type of empathy as only they can do!

Along with birth position, preferred pain relief (or not), and any other paraphernalia required for labour, today this can be recorded in a birth plan. To Martians, the meaning is different. A true birth plan has to be achievable. For Venetian, it's a wish list. By taking the Venetian approach, conflicts can quickly arise as Martians do not understand how difficult it can be just to say, 'I want that one'. On the basis that the Venetians' hormones are decidedly all over the show, our displays of irritation can be taken as either disinterested or non-supportive. Nope, it's just the inherent frustration and an unfortunate side-effect of living with another creature that looks the same but definitely has a mind wired completely differently. Martians missed the lesson on being tactful when matters do not quite go as planned. Before leaving Mars, they rushed off too quickly when they noticed how lovely Venetians were and forgot to build up resilience to not overreact to repetitive sentences such as 'What do you think about this idea?'

All the 'what to do' during labour books resurface. The Google engine is stoked up, and any other browser you can think of is given the key search words. 'What can you include in a birth plan?' Returning to the circle of chairs at the ante-natal classes, all try and put their ideas forward. Or do they? This is one time when the mothers-to-be become rather cagey so as not to entirely reveal what they are planning in the hope no one else has the same idea! We say goodbye to just lying on the back and pushing, which has worked well for centuries, in preference to the latest thoughts on what is needed in labour and to form part of the birth plan. A potential first entry is aromatherapy.

"Look here, love…apparently, the evidence from this study I searched suggests that aromatherapy, as complementary and alternative labour assistance, can help in relieving maternal anxiety and pain during labour. It requires the application of essential oils to relax and control the mind and body through aromatic compounds and essential oils that calm the nerves and any aches or pains," she spoke.

"Mmm, really?" He said (But thinking in silence, what a load of tosh).

She went on, "Perhaps I should consider what they suggest and have the oils in the birth room. Well, once I have decided where this will be, home or hospital," she said. (although he was thinking, What about on top of Mount Everest…Give me strength).

On looking at the type of oils and the specific benefits it breaks down to this:

Lavender Oil: promotes relaxation and eases muscular tension.
Frankincense Oil: calms your emotions by inhaling the aroma.
Peppermint Oil: can ease nausea during labour by inhaling the aroma.
Jasmine Oil: evokes feelings of joy, happiness, peace and self-confidence.

The Martians' thoughts are turned to what they do best. What the hell are these oils, and where can you acquire them? If my darling believes they would help, then who am I to question? Eek. The only reference most people would have heard as to the availability of where you would obtain frankincense was when one of the three kings was bearing such a gift to baby Jesus. Clearly, having the wonder oil after baby Jesus was born was a bit late. It would have been more helpful if Mary had the frankincense to calm her nerves when giving birth in the cow shed due to her useless husband Joseph being too late on 'TripAdvisor' to find a decent hotel for the census in Bethlehem. Going by the Monty Python parody 'Life of Brian' it couldn't be that valuable, as when their three kings found out they had gone to welcome a 'Brian' instead of Jesus, they only wanted the gold present returned in their quest to locate the correct Messiah.

Can you imagine setting up all these essential oils in a hospital? Staff rushing around whilst you are asking which room is yours. From experience with the lack of resources, the chance of securing a facility in advance is next to no chance. What if your birth experience would be one of those extremely fast deliveries?

"Hold on, dear. I know that you are now eight centimetres dilated, but could you just hold off for a few minutes while I set up the essential oils you wanted on the windowsill and for me to obtain the fire disclaimer form to light up the joss stick for you? I must deliver the birth plan for you, darling," he would say.

We all have different music tastes, but in childbirth, it takes on a new meaning under the guise 'Music Therapy'. If you think it would be a recognisable genre, then you would be wrong. Apparently, from another Google Search, we have a new profession. That of a music therapist. These folks can be certified (certified mad, in my opinion) and employed. As such, structured musical interventions can be provided to relieve anxiety and pain during and after childbirth.

The most preferred musical sounds are reported as being soft selections. Peaceful and calming music, which normally includes nature sounds. The claimed benefits (which were not explained) are to increase oxytocin and beta-endorphins, which help with moving labour forward and 'pain management'. (A new term that will appear quite frequently in any well-crafted birth plan.)

Imagine an old-time musical theatre organ in the corner of the delivery room. It's being played by some therapist in a glitzy show outfit spinning his head and smiling away with his tombstone teeth as he pumps out whale music to the intensity of the contractions. As the baby rears itself at the tip of the birth canal, he changes to a musical crescendo with an array of flashing lights on the Wurlitzer. The full birth is given the Ryanair treatment as if an aeroplane has landed on time with triumphant horns and a congratulatory cacophony of harmonic singing.

Breathing techniques are obvious. The mainstay of self-help in my mother's ante-natal classes. What could have changed? Well, funnily enough, it starts simply enough: 'Breathe in through your nose and sigh out through the mouth'. But no. The modern recommended step is to "breathe in through your nose and imagine, as you sigh out, that you are causing a candle flame to gently flicker. It may also be useful to greet the contraction with a sigh and end with a sigh."

Whilst all the techniques require practice, the steps for a J-breath could be difficult or a potential moment of hysterical laughter. The J-method is all about releasing your pelvic floor and letting your baby move naturally down the birth canal, i.e., do not hold your breath but let the old bugger move naturally. The Google post states, 'The best time to practice this is on the toilet when having a poop. Take a deep, deep breath in and out as you release your bowels, blow through your mouth, and imagine the breath travelling down your intestines and out of your bottom!'

This would be one instance of a pain management technique where a Martian would want to be entirely excused. It's hard to know what sort of encouragement could be given standing beside the pan.

'Come on, squeeze that shit out like after a Friday night curry!'

If Martians are to become the breathing coach they would, of course, be tasked to seek what this would entail in practice. Another dip into the 'birth library' or as revealed with a browse on 'Google', highlights that timing of the breathing can assist in determining the length of contraction. One could learn to breathe at the same rate as the mum-to-be ensuring that focus can be maintained throughout labour with the intention of providing a state of euphoric relaxation.

A Venetian birth partner would undoubtedly be more empathetic with their repertoire by reminding her of that special phrase, not forgetting to hold their hand or offer sips of water but men would tend to fall back to type and relish the far more technical support role. The timing of the breathing would be by way of a stopwatch and a chart attached to an old-fashioned clipboard. Each breath could then be monitored as to the exact time for each set. The support to the mother would include the accompanying breathing technique to be mimicked. Great delight and importance to the role would be attached in advising whether the last timed breath was too long or short. Once in a while, the discerning Martian would provide more detail as to the mid-term practice trend.

Allegedly, this should help release endorphins (the body's own natural pain reliever) and ease the discomfort of the contractions when the time comes. Okay, so no pain-killing substances are required if the birth partner performs well with the coaching.

The other interesting matter was the suggested phrases that could be used for the purposes of this pain management technique:

- *Hang in There! This phrase provides a note of support without a lot of pressure.*
- *I Love You.*
- *Think of the Baby*
- *You're Going to Be a Great Mother*
- *Awesome!*
- *Keep Going*
- *Just a Bit More*
- *You Are Doing It!*

It wasn't really what would be on a Martian's schedule of helpful phrases as the focus would be on what they thought a mum-to-be would want to hear:

"Imagine walking along a sandy beach hewn out of golden flakes with a gentle breeze wisping in and out of your nose and mouth."

Or in reverse:

"C'mon, you badass. Push the flecking thing out. You know in two hours, the England football team is playing in the last World Cup group decider."

In the quest for a birth experience of a lifetime, the alpha mums may consider a water-borne affair. All the different magazines, such as 'Best Mum', 'Pregnancy Monthly', and 'Nine Months and Counting' magazines, include various women in full-colour exhibiting the latest trend of wallowing in the wet stuff as the new fashion in labour is extracted from the pile. Martians would still be invited to enter the debate although his role from here on in would be both as an observer and purportedly a degree of support in the way that would be offered on Venus, "What about a water birth?" She said.

Gulp. "What's one of them?" Is the man's immediate reaction.

"Haven't you read all those articles and magazines I have given you? I would like this method in my birth plan."

A lesson learnt from Dr Gray's metaphor is to consider what you say before murmuring any response. Rather than saying, "Why the hell would you want a water birth?" Instead, modify it to a kinder verbal exchange of, "If you really want a water birth, you go ahead, dear, and look into it. Let me know once you have decided."

The first key element of considering a water birth for the plan was to source the facility. Although the National Health Service continues to move forward, it cannot be assumed each maternity unit has a birthing pool. If it has, it is extremely unlikely that there would be more than one. If not, is a room available that can be used should you be able to hire a pool? For the sake of argument, let's assume it is possible only in one, delivery room seven.

What is unknown is whether this room is permanently empty or multi-use for any birth. On hearing a mum-to-be wanted a water birth, staff would need to chalk up on the status blackboard above the nurse station that an incoming was approaching. Get the porters and remove the static beds. Clear the gangway, a 'portable' water pool is in view, being dragged down the corridor by a reluctant Martian.

The conundrum sows a seed of doubt in the man's mind as to the likelihood that a water birth remains a realistic proposition. What would be the circumstance if room seven had already been allocated to another woman? You can hardly puncture the pool that the other mother is using so you can muscle in. Alternatively, one could consider putting a proposal forward for the loan of their DIY facility. Taking a few more seconds to ruminate, is it realistic to re-use the now murky waters?

Can all midwives carry out a water birth? Apparently not. They have to have a 'special' status, which is only gained after a number of 'assists' under the belt. Is there a health and safety protocol that has to include lifeguard training? Probably requiring refresher courses every six months to keep up to speed with submerging techniques to extract the baby from the wallowing solution and stop the mother from drowning.

Thus, the likelihood of achieving this method already relies on a DIY birthing pool, the availability of a 'suitable' labour room, and where an experienced midwife is on duty. Sadly, this is not the end of factors requiring consideration.

"At the last attempt, the water was so brown I could not see the baby's head. If the water does not return to a colour that you would normally expect, i.e., clear, then any midwife would not be prepared to continue for the sake of you and your baby's safety. Oh, and by the way, if you want any painkillers or need to have an induced labour, you cannot have a water birth either," the duty matron piped up.

This is a mere challenge to any Venetian and, with no hesitation, continues to stick with water birth as the preferred go-to method for the 'birth plan'.

The Martian, whilst being a doubting Thomas, sets out a strategy to source the said DIY pool. After all, it is a welcome distraction being a practical mission whilst portraying to the birth mum that no expense would be spared and remain positive to meet her birth plan. Various companies would be short-listed. It was not just price but length of hire (in case the baby was late) and, of course, the free accompanying accessories that were to be offered. In this story, the chosen company could also provide a pump, a seat to be placed in the pool (Who for?), various hoses, a thermometer, and a 'precision' sieve. The sieve is required to mine sweep any undesirable detritus material languishing in the pool during and after labour. Definitely not fishing for the catch of the day.

The equipment would need to be supplemented from home to include tools that you would have to second guess as to what they may be used for. A torch would be essential, assuming the water was discolouring. A mirror, possibly to reflect the light from the torch towards the expanding cervix, and finally, a condom (a bit late now). The 'Johnny' would be needed to ensure that the sound monitor could be kept dry. Apparently, the NHS could not stretch to this added expense.

The next dilemma was the size of the birth pool and how collapsible it would be. As occurs quite frequently, women and men have varying ideologies of how the experience would play out. Her concept was that the birth partner should join her in the pool. Whereas from the male perspective, it would be to stand dotingly at the side, giving support, shouting instructions, and acting as a glorified pool attendant. So, size does matter, and with the Martian's greater knowledge of estimating the dimensions of anything (apart from one male instrument!) plumped for the smallest unit he could find. With that situation in mind, should a new pair of goggles and flippers be acquired to be all ready to dive into that pool to inspect for any leakage or to ensure the pump is working satisfactorily? What swimming trunks should be worn? Perhaps an all-in-one stripy number or a blue boiler suit supporting a name tag as to his position of responsibility. Should one pack a diving belt to attach the infamous sieve to go fishing for anything that appears in the water other than the baby?

The hiring of the water birth equipment normally needs to be around two weeks before the due date. Do not be fooled by the hire literature, which states, "The pool and all the necessary accompanying 'tools' should fit comfortably into a small car." One would have thought this would include a Mercedes family saloon and that only the boot space would be necessary. From a practical perspective, this is always a comfort for Martians. They despise having clutter on the passenger seats, as it gives the impression of a very disorganised planetary being. It would also have a practical dimension that one could leave all the paraphernalia securely locked away in readiness for the dash to the maternity unit.

When the collection day arrives, all will be revealed as to what actually has been hired. Being presented with a very large and heavy rectangular box, which one could barely grab, even with outstretched arms, and by a quick estimate, you concur with yourself, 'Yes' it will fit in the boot of the car. Thus, a logical presumption that it's a moment to thank the company employee and wave goodbye:

"There's more yet, mate. There are another five boxes like that one!" He said.

Martians must never assume that advertising is correct. The 'will fit in a small car' was limited to the payload of a station wagon. A saloon Mercedes is no delivery van, but somebody either cannot estimate sizes or, having hired so many to dumbfounded Martians who do not want to make a fuss, knew that nine out of ten of these men would not even pass the slightest comment when faced with such an embarrassment that you have not met the planetary code of being correct.

Looking at the enormity of the jigsaw pieces now collected, most males would have in mind a dry run (so to speak). Imagine the day of the birth without such a practice. Flexing muscles and drawing breath, it was time to tackle the 'kit for a small car,' extracting the six boxes from the vehicle. The individual pieces could only just be manhandled through the front door without taking the frame with them. Not a good start thinking of dragging the elements through the maternity unit to delivery suite seven.

Stage one of the pre-trial was to locate a flat area of sufficient size. The kitchen floor is always a fair choice if tiled, as would best typify the likely texture of the space in delivery suite number seven. The individual boxes positioned around the sides of the cupboard units provided something familiar akin to a sheep pen.

A Martian would plan to re-use the sticky tape binding material on the removal of the pool panels from the boxes. Hire companies always bind boxes with vigour and exponentially with more care than the service offered. You know the stuff. If you rip it off, it takes the whole side of the cardboard with it as well if not handled carefully. It also has a mind of its' own. Unravelling until it comes into contact with another piece where it would stop dead. Stuck together like shit to a blanket. As an aside, a useful study that could be carried out on Mars would be to test the braking strain of each brand of binding material. My money would be on any tape derivative that the hire company had used with its name printed on it in all its glory. The reel repeats with the telephone number just in case it slipped your mind. 'BIRTHWORKS TEL: 001437 234923' was sure to be the winner.

The sticky tape problem eventually turned into an asset. By carefully cutting and removing where it had overlapped, sufficient binding strips could be kept to enable the boxes to be later resealed without needing to find a new roll. This is always a long task in itself in any joint household. Indeed, the practice of repacking large bulky boxes is a skill learnt by Martians on Earth, as they are invariably called upon to repack and send back in the post any unwanted goods purchased by Venetians.

The first component to pull out was the blue rubbery liner. Those on Venus believe 'cleanliness is next to godliness' when it comes to any material that might come into contact with skin. There was going to be no wallowing in the birthing pool where another person had positioned their buttocks in the crease of the blue liner. Having been explained as to when the sieve would need to be called upon, one could understand the concern. To guarantee no awkwardness, a throw-away liner would also be needed.

It is amazing the faith one puts in anything offered for hire must surely be fit for purpose, but today an assumption which is misplaced. The hexagonal sheets of heavy plywood, which were the route of both handling and inflexibility, did not give confidence in a smooth construction on the day of the birth. There were no hinges, flex joints, or inserts, but instead (you've guessed it) just sticky tape. Not the same as the packaging tape but an inferior black tape that had already deteriorated to such a point there was no worry of sticking to your fingers.

What do you do? Take it back? Complain only to receive an occasional and inane 'sorry' where the sound of the 'r' is lengthened in that the meaning is expressed as sarcasm, where what is actually meant is "I don't give a flying fig of what you think. You have paid and will use any excuse not for you to either request an exchange or refund."

This is where the planet's code of purchasing and acquisition ethics diverge. Those from Venus are naturally more ready and able to take up the challenge that if perfection has not been delivered, retribution is required. Even if the easier route is to mend and make do. Venetian tongues are designed differently. Not physically but metaphorically, where they have the ability to extend and create a whip effect that can take out the eye, ears and then wrap around a service provider's throat if recompense and a full apology are not forthcoming. The constant 'giving-in' by Martians, as Venetians would see it, severely dents our masculinity, but given the chance, men would always take the route of least resistance.

As such, the equipment needed for the 'Pool Maintenance Kit' grew to include make-do and mend items for the vagaries of the birth facility. A roll of duct tape to repair and fit the blue liner, which was not very pliable, being comparable to a lorry weather tarpaulin, and a rubber mallet to smash those lugs to fix the panels. The now bulging tool bag ran to more items than the bleeding birthing bag. The 'holdall' for the big day now included a sieve, torch, handheld mirror, bucket, retractable DIY knife, condom, backup thermometer, spare batteries (torch and tens machine), goggles, flippers (optional), and snorkel (optional).

The Martian could now report that after the pool trial, leaving out any hint of a struggle, erecting a water birthing facility was doable, confirming its inclusion in the plan.

One could write an entire book of what should or should not be included in any discerning birth plan, but worth providing a fictitious example one could imagine would be the go-to preconditions for an alpha Venetian. The unrepentant belief remains, of course, that such a plan, the whole plan, and nothing other than the whole plan would be completely deliverable.

AN ALPHA VENETIAN BIRTH PLAN

BIRTH PARTNER

- *Will be my husband, XXX. (Or Wife)*
- *I would prefer not to have students or any such audience in attendance at the delivery for my special*

and precious moment. (Assuming it will be as dreamt!)

LABOUR-if Possible, I Would Like To...

- *Keep upright and active during labour.*
- *Have access to a birthing pool.*
- *I would like to use a portable stereo to play music to relax/distract me using the soundtrack so lovingly compiled by my birth partner.*
- *I am also interested in the possibility of using aromatherapy by means of essential oils.*

PAIN RELIEF

As my starting gambit is '*I WANT A WATER BIRTH*'. I have noted that no pain relief can be administered. If, and only if I indicate by me hollering with extreme pain I would want to scale up in the following order:

- *Use a TENS machine.*
- *Encouraged to use breathing techniques and various positions to cope with the contractions.*
- *Use gas and air.*
- *Use Diamorphine or Pethidine or similar if becomes very uncomfortable.*
- *I would prefer not to have Epidural. But will take advice if close to passing out.*

THE BIRTH

- *Try giving birth in the birthing pool.*
- *I would prefer every effort to be made to avoid having an episiotomy.*
- *I would prefer every effort to be made to avoid tearing.*
- *At intervals, I should like monitoring with a handheld Sonic aid. My birth partner has packed the rubber sheath for the purpose of the use underwater.*
- *I would prefer that vent house or forceps be avoided.*
- *I would prefer that a Caesarean Section be performed only in exceptional circumstances.*
- *My birth partner XXXX would like to cut the umbilical cord.*
- *I would like to try breastfeeding the baby straightaway.*

AFTER THE BIRTH

- *If I have to be stitched, I would prefer a senior midwife or doctor to carry this out and not a trainee.*
- *If available, I would like the use of a side room.*

GENERAL

I would very much like it if I was attended to by the midwives that I have met during pregnancy. I appreciate logistics could mean that this is not possible but after all this is my birth plan. Failing the NHS cannot meet this request I would like the midwife in attendance to be good with her instruction and experience in all midwifery events so that I

109

*may take clear guidance from her to enable me to feel
confident with my delivery and have as safer birth as can be
expected given any unforeseen circumstances.*

Hindsight is a wonderful expression. A wise Martian
would say that there remained no need to consider casting
back over the last few months and thinking 'If only' when the
birth plan was never going to see the light of day. This
situation ordinarily could be very much a 'I told you so'
moment. However, this is a particular instance where the
situation commands restraint in what he thinks and what he
would very much like to say. This unique moment for any
couple when a new life comes into this mad world remains a
very special celebration.

As smugly predicted in the Martians thoughts, the details
and expectations of most birth plans are never going to happen
in a month of Sundays.

There was ever only an outside chance that the DIY pool
facility would see the light of day. Having the whole suite of
painkillers was always on the cards, and what is wrong with
that? It is no defeat to limit the pain. Who could blame a mum
in labour for taking the tried and tested position on their back?
Not on their knees, not with one leg at one hundred and eighty
degrees or the crouch position against a wall. The
practicalities of ever setting up a portable stereo player are
marginal. A quick eyeball around any delivery room would
confirm a limited number of available electric sockets to
justify lugging the machine into the delivery suite. All those
hours and hours spent compiling various sounds, including
whales, birds tweeting from the garden, and the swishing of
trees in the wind for the purpose, become time that could have

been far better utilised, like being down the pub with fellow Martians and ye olde expression of 'Watching paint dry'.

When it came to the male support role to whisper the sweet words of encouragement as specified in the birth plan, how many instances are they greeted with an impolite stare that would scare the most hardened criminal with the clear message to 'Just shut up'?

The one piece of hi-tech pain-relieving tool is barely fit for purpose. The Tens machine. The sticky pads on the electrodes are clearly not designed for a sweaty back during labour. Do they offer much pain relief to those mums wanting to avoid an injection? Nah. Confirmed after a few minutes passing to 'Yes, yes, yes, yes…yes please, please. Bloody any pain killer you have'.

A Martian's choice for any birth plan would be pretty unlikely to include electing to cut the umbilical cord.

This is a Venetian alpha's requirement as a poetic wish and an instance where its inclusion is not queried at the time in the hope that the law of averages is played out where such a situation does not transpire or gets forgotten.

Why would any Venetian believe it would be at the front of his mind. One can only assume it is something Venetians would consider, and would they really believe their man would spout the following request:

"Oh yes, dear. I have a specific requirement for the birth plan. I would like to cut the umbilical cord. It's something I have dreamt of doing since a child!"

Martians can also have a tinge of embarrassment that they have somewhat been complicit in the formulation of the birth plan. That of the alpha mum believing that they have any control over the maternity ward operational logistics for their birth. With human nature as it is, I doubt the general 'wishes' would be taken in the spirit as they have been presented if viewed by the health professionals. Imagine the more than likely scenario where the midwife 'A' team could not be rallied as requested but instead the attendant mid-wife is unknown to the birth parents.

"Oh. Is this your birth plan? I do apologise that I wasn't the mid-wife you were hoping for. I will try and do the best I can, having only seen babies being delivered in a class, and that was out of a Clarks pink shoe box."

In the final analysis, Martians would much prefer the plan to stay in the birthing bag and to only become tomorrow's chip paper. From asking the same question over and over again of other couples, there has been no instance of anyone pulling out the infernal birth plan from a bag or pocket. Or indeed, even from a tacit recollection to follow the step-by-step labour wishes as the birth progresses.

When all said and done, the assertion is arguably that most Venetians would also secretly agree that a scribed birth plan has a very diminished value once the wave of emotion and pain management is to the fore. This leads to forgetting all the pre-planning where it only gets remembered when a crumpled and sodden sheet of paper is pulled from the bottom of the birthing bag when the whole experience quickly becomes ancient history.

Chapter 9
The First Few Days

The days after the birth of the special one can be a real strain on the new parents. The dawn of a new life and the changing dynamics of the family. There is no denying the euphoria as to the gift of life for both planetary beings. However, the approaches and priorities can be diametrically different, or at least create a more than unique set of misunderstandings.

For example. Who gets to see the newborn first? To Martians, this is a practical conundrum. Who lives the closest to the birth location and can make the time slot for when the first visits are permitted. Unbeknownst to the Martian, plans for the 'popping in to view rota' had already been decided and agreed beforehand with various dwellers of their planet. No discussion is ever had with the dad but just presented with the order. There is a priority sequence in which the first is the mother of the birth mother. He may wonder why his mum is relegated to the second division but dares not intervene. It's a 'fait accompli'. If Mum's mum is not available due to a very unlikely situation, an assortment of ifs and buts come into play based on 'substitutes' and 'reserves' from the Venetian list, which still may not include the dad's mum. Mars man's attitude remains unphased as to who sees the child from a premier position over the coming weeks. It is a distraction. The nimblest of men see such a debate as best to be avoided, bearing in mind what is to come. Firstly, as the baby leaves the hospital.

Clothes. What outfit should be worn? The decision is not one that is made based on the most practical factors, such as the baby's size, but on the source of the clothes. It could be that the Mum's Mum gave it as a present, as she demanded it be the first article worn on leaving the hospital. This, of course, was bought for a twelve- to eighteen-month-old baby to ensure sufficient growing size for longevity of use. The zero to six months correct size is put back in the birthing bag. The cardigan knitted by a close aunt and sent from overseas must be worn, enabling photos to demonstrate to the Venetian compatriot that even though sweat is dripping off the baby's brow as it is the height of summer, her attire has the accolade of first dibs.

Photo shoots. Every angle has to be considered. Thank any god for small mercies that this did not have to include legs in stirrups on the delivery table, a cavernous vagina, or a baby's head covered in vernix. Mars dwellers do not see the value of hundreds of shots that never see the light of day but are constantly reminded that one has to click away at every and any opportunity. The request is always carried out for the sake of harmony, but it is difficult not to show a facial grimace of contempt. The man gets given the task if the birth mum is unable to get the desired angle on the journey from the delivery suite to the ward or when the Venetian's phone has reached its memory capacity. No picture out of the many can be deleted. It's now the turn of his camera memory to be filled to the brim.

Off he has to trot to all those special places. Sideward, the actual delivery room, the corridor where the first cuddle with the baby was had on the way to the recovery room, all the health team (including the janitor), every bleeding one of them. Then we have the visits (from the first division), the first outfit, the walk out to the car, into the car, and so on. The greatest absentee is the father. Men are quite up for the first pictures with the baby and mum. Enough to show their own planetary colleagues of their presence during the birthing experience. But when it comes to a constant flow, they begrudgingly agree to the minimum of appearances so as not to disappoint. They really prefer the concept of always being behind the camera or smartphone rather than in front of it.

The next situation of potential attrition is the car journey home from the maternity unit. Mars man excels at practical solutions. The positioning of the car seat is second nature. This is known by Venetians but does not stop the comment, 'Have you put the car seat in correctly?' Such a remark can infuriate Martians as they accept that before such a task is implemented, they are more than willing to refer to 'The Instructions'. These are accepted as essential on Mars for any new situation, but the concept is uncommon and decidedly rare on Venus. Their mantra is to have a go first, then regroup when a problem arises. This manifests in having to request assistance, which usually consists of asking a Martian. Of course, the immediate reaction to the annoyance of the Venetians is for him to enquire as to whether reference to the instructions has occurred. Apparently not, as the sound of rummaging is heard in the bin as they are retrieved. Once the baby is now firmly anchored into the baby carriage, the next request is for journey intelligence.

"What will be the direction of the sun on the drive home?" She spoke.

The natural reaction would be to serve back with a negative response of, "I don't bleeding know. Who do you think I am, a meteorologist as well as an orienteering guide?"

But make sure you know what you intend to say so as not to put a dampener on this day of firsts.

"It is really hard to tell, darling. It depends on which way we travel home, whether the clouds lift, and where the sun will shine through. Let's just put a sun shade front, back, and sideways, but leave sufficient space the size of a letter on the windscreen so I can still peer out to drive while ensuring all the bases are covered," he diplomatically states.

The home visit rota is now being organised. For Venetians, it is an opportunity to show close friends and family that they should be just as proud as what was the result of the nine months in transit of the Dauphine or Dauphin.

There are very few mums in this world who believe their baby is not the prettiest, most handsome, or has the best features from toes to nose compared to any other child that has ever been born. It is quite ironic to observe conversations regarding whatever hair is present on the head, even a single strand, wondering if the baby has the best style ever and when the first haircut should be arranged!

The Martian view is, yep, they are just as proud as a Venetian, but with an absence of any competitive dialogue to suggest one's own cherub may be superior to any other. In the words of the 'Plusnet' Telecom company slogan: 'That will do'. This reaction can confuse a Venetian into thinking a Martian is not as overwhelmed. Restraint of one's emotions in this situation is common on Mars. What is also foreign for the Martians is the need for group affirmation as the home visits commence. No additional endorsement is necessary.

As various well-wishers are paraded in view of the newborn, held aloft in swaddling clothes, the thought turns to the most complimentary reaction that can be mustered. This is given assistance by clothing the baby in as many gift items that could conceivably be fitted, which could run to five layers, so the following comment is elicited:

"Don't they just look the best in that outfit/ hat/ booties/ jumper/ cardigan that I chose? I have never seen such a lovely baby."

Rather than:

"Didn't you like that outfit/hat/booties/jumper/cardigan that I chose?"

You would never class putting a baby to bed as being on top of a 'best practice' agenda, but apparently so. It is quite understandable to take all precautions against the phenomenon of cot death, but at some point, common sense needs to prevail. The perspective is often different where Venetian research takes regard to every piece of advice, although some remain conflicting. The corollary of this situation results in both sexes coming up with different solutions to maintain the baby's well-being.

Which way should a baby sleep: back, front or side? Whatever position is agreed upon, how should this be executed? Since the early nineties, it's been recommended to put your baby on their back for every sleep, day and night. Okay, got it. So, what method should be used to ensure the baby doesn't move? Well, the Mars option is to create some form of wedge on either side of the baby so that they cannot roll. While logical, some advice is not to use anything that could constrict movement.

Should the baby indeed move to the side or front, which, let's face it, is quite likely, then you intervene, turning once again so the bum is back down on the cot mattress and belly up.

We have again the dilemma of taking the advice in the literal sense. Standing and watching over the baby all night. This is likely to be the alpha mums' course of action. The males would be content with two rolled-up blankets on either side of the cot. I can imagine a Martian's practical ingenuity coming to the fore to save an all-night awakening. One might be a form of baby toe tag with a bell. Any movement to the side would bring about a ring, ding, ding, requiring an intervention to straighten the torso.

During sleep, the items of clothing need to be of sufficient quantity to ensure the baby is comfortable. A baby that is too hot could be susceptible to overheating. Too cold, and they could become baby blue. The Martian way of practical monitoring is to use the back of the hand on the chest or head to gauge the baby's temperature. This procedure was good enough for the preceding five hundred years, but apparently it is now not deemed an acceptable method on Venus. Reference has to be to the 'Tog' guide.

This is a list provided by the health visitor. It also appeared in many of the monthly magazines that, as any Martian knows, had been added to since the pre-birth periodicals, which remained scattered around the home in the hope Martians would pick up and flick through.

Each item of clothing would have its own unique value, ranging from a half to two. The objective was to get as close to a tog value of ten as possible. Most would do an estimate and attain an approximation to the general warmth layer required. However, this would not be acceptable to the alpha mum. A list would have to be made, or for the most sophisticated of alphas, a spreadsheet for the week's attire. Maybe even a plan for the entire month. All the individual items identified as being of potential use during the period would be listed on the sheet, including the ascribed 'tog' value. A pencil, paper, and eraser from the olden days remain useful for this exercise, but to ensure absolute accuracy, an electronic calculator would be called for. Thus, each item laid out could be ticked off to include the vest, baby-grow, sleepsuit, and blankets for the nighttime to get to the magical figure of ten and attain the optimum comfortable temperature.

There is a slight flaw for the alpha mum. That is the tog value pertaining to nappies and the degree of nappy soiling one should include. If the paper pulp is assumed to be completely dry through the night, then this layer would count as a fifth of a point on the old tog scale. On becoming wet, the warmth factor would reduce to a tenth, and for a good old shit, the moist and succulent compound would double the tog. Thus, an alpha dilemma is created so as to hit the absolute mark, unless one is prepared to stay up all night and wait for a piddle or poo. It really becomes implausible to be that exact, however one tries.

The advice for nighttime in all the 'baby manuals' does not end there and fuels the recipe for planetary conflict as to how the 'Rules' must be followed. Martians are more likely to see these 'dos' and 'do nots' as a guide, and common sense should prevail. This does not appear the same on Venus.

When the 'Dad' takes his turn to return the baby to bed, such as after a feed or a change of soiled nappies, he immediately goes back to type. He completely forgets he is supposed to follow the tog warmth value method of calculation as the back of the hand is manoeuvred onto that exposed bit of pink flesh around the face. Yep, that seems fine; with full knowledge, mum is snoring like a bear in the next-door bedroom after a hard day's mothering.

He also does not seem to quite master the tucking in or the correct distance for the feet away from the bottom of the cot. Apparently, the books and guidance say (along with no cot bumper) that the feet must be no further than one inch (two and a half centimetres) from the bottom of the bed.

When cot rest time was decided by the alpha, even if dad was assigned the duty, on any occasion, Mum could not resist double-checking quality control. What occurs to the Martian is that she may have put the baby to bed herself. The Martian would yet again feel emancipated and have to practice a tight grip of his teeth to get through the moment without venting his spleen into a 'sod off, I'm dealing with this and fully capable without needing an inspection from you'.

So here comes the lecture after the methodology audit, a huff, and the leading question of the dad in an attempt to diffuse the situation with, 'How do you want me to do it then?' (In your perfect Venetian world, he thinks.)

"Well, I would have measured the exact length of the baby and have got a ruler out so that when fully stretched, his feet are correct to the bottom of the cot." Dad continues to listen intently.

"Then I would lay the blankets and make sure that they came up to just below his shoulder. Thereafter, every time I put him back to bed, I know that if the blankets are tucked in properly (Mum emphasis), our cherub will always be returned to the advised position as written down in the manuals you are supposed to be following."

With that, Dad would of course be seething inside but retorts instead, "Perhaps from now on, Mum, you better take control of all the night feeds, nappy changing, and any other child caring."

"Just do as you are told!" Was the bite back, and with that, the Martian took a side step for the greater good and gently placed the scale rule now in his possession by the side of the cot so as to give the impression the 'House rules' will now be followed without question.

This exemplifies yet again each gender's approach to child care. Both partners have the child's welfare at heart but just tackle the 'how' from different perspectives. The method of the Venetian is considered too exacting by Martians, where their way represents a more practical application of techniques that still amount to the same outcome honed through thousands of years of judging the level of input that is required for a task on Mars. Venetians perceive the Martian's way as too casual and spawned out of laziness, which can lead to fractious parenting. If both sexes understood why each took a different approach and actually acknowledged that both viewpoints are fine, the stress levels would be far, far lower.

When this does not happen, we have the following recurring 'Snipes' lists:

The Martian's book of phrases

"Don't fuss, he's all right."

"I have just checked his temperature my way and I know he is fine."

"Just because I don't do XXXX the way you want me to that doesn't mean my method is wrong."

"I'm sure other parents don't do it as precisely as you do."

"My mum never did it that way with my siblings and we all survived."

"If you won't let me look after him my way then do it yourself."

The Venetian's comparative list

"I am just checking you have done XXXX correctly."

"If you would just pick up one of those magazines, or read the research on the browser you would understand why we have to look after baby exactly this way."

"If you cared as much as I do, you would do as I ask."

"What was acceptable then is not now. They really didn't know what they were doing and now we have all the proven research to change."

"Who gave birth? You or me?"

The way both genders approach practical parenting can manifest into a state of stereotypical repetition of the first few days. That is a different ideology that is prone to conflict. Those from Venus focus on a belt and braces application in most situations. Thus, ensuring all angles are covered so the baby does not reach a point of reduced comfortability. On the other hand, men are prone to make a fine judgement in that less intervention has more weight in certain situations, such as when a nappy requires replacing.

Both genders predict when a change may be necessary. The problem arises because each planet has different scales or gauges. Martians work in a near full situation. The clasping of the hand around the nappy with a little shake gives the assurance that it is near to full and that a longer period of elapsed time is still possible to attain a 'comfortable' maximum. It is then and only then that a Martian is satisfied that, although a slight whimpering from the child is registered, it is the right time to augment a replacement. However, this approach is unfamiliar to those from Venus. There is no such weight test. The decision is based on looking at the baby for any hint of discomfort. It may not be even a cry, but it is an extra sensory measure of how the baby feels that has never been available on Mars. The decision is immediately taken that the nappy must be wet or soiled with poo of various consistency and colours that you could identify on a 'hints of brown' paint shade sample chart. Off it comes, and a new one is placed over the peachy bum. When the top-up of supplies becomes necessary, conflict could arise.

"I can't believe how many nappies our little one gets through each week," she said.

"I do. You are changing the nappies far too often and before necessary. When I have seen your discarded nappies in the bin, they are not fully wet and could have been left on for longer," he states.

"Really, are you so tight you would let our little cherub suffer in silence with a soggy bum?"

"Don't be an ignoramus. Of course, I wouldn't. If matey was that bothered, he would be crying out loud."

Or.

The approach to the same situation when the wiser Martian had now started to acquire knowledge from the lessons learnt would be:

"I can't believe how many nappies our little one gets through each week," she said.

His measured response is now simply, "Yeah, it's simply amazing," He retorts, taking one for the team!

As a potentially typical occurrence, there is a difference between a two-parent family made up solely of Venetians. There is calmness. No debate occurs as to whether it is the right time to discard and renew. If anything, the conflict only comes about when they can't decide whose turn it is to strip and change. There is, however, a potential weakness for a two-female partnership. Men naturally revel in their logistical and practical prowess, such as the tightness with which one affixes the tabs to stop leakage for the next time. It is an art to get the tension just right. They quickly learn that the tighter the better, and the best check is to see a little imprint on the waistband as one would have with a new sock around the ankle. The preferred Venetian approach is to follow a far more delicate strategy so as to ensure there is no chance of any distress to the baby. This calls for a looser fit between the nappy and body and could lead to a leakage disaster pretty soon after the change. And normally, at the point when the baby is handed to the adoring grandparents!

The above exchanges tell us that men do not like to be challenged as to whether they are doing a task correctly. It doesn't happen on Mars. One can ask politely with such expressions as 'Are you okay with that' or 'Let us know if you need anything' but not a direct challenge. A good example, as we heard from the mum earlier in this tale, was the expression, 'Have you strapped our cherub correctly in the car seat?' Have Venetians not learnt anything either since zooming down to planet Earth that a variance in their methods can potentially cause disquiet during further parenting experiences?

Chapter 10
Why Can't Dads Understand Doting Mums

It's fascinating how Venetians have an apparent closer affectionate bond with babies and children than their male counterparts. Martians do not react in an instant to every twitch and flinch. There is a more measured approach before any interventions are deemed necessary in the care of the baby. This gives the impression that the paternal instincts of the average man are not as intense. This could not be further from the truth. It is a phenomenon that needs consideration as to whether love is any different or stronger between the genders or indeed planets.

It would seem perverse to contemplate a 'scale' towards the depth of love between the sexes, as the outward pouring of warmth can be impacted by any domestic situation. Many males vocalise less and digest in our inner sanctum what we truly feel. Pride and protectionism are actually not that different.

Many Martians' public displays of affection are reserved for tangible milestone events. Venetians have different training. Their manual prescribes a very unrestrained holler from every roof top as to what exactly is being felt or, for that matter, being thought. No holding back for any emotional event accompanied by telling all and talking, talking and talking. It's a difference in such practical applications of feeling that can lead to a very real misunderstanding.

A common situation is the quest to establish any perceived discomfort in the child, which ultimately becomes a constant crusade. Martians can view such a mantra as pretty irritating. Their general opinion is to consider a tangible and significant change in the set of circumstances that present themselves. It is understood that all bases need to be covered regarding a fairly typical baby checklist of comfort. Firstly, is he hungry? Then, in order of priority, Is the baby wet or is there any evidence of a poo? Perhaps he or she needs more sleep? Is he possibly ill? If these are all satisfactorily checked off, a Martian would assume a sufficient state of well-being exists. Anything else is classed as a 'winge' and at 3:00 am in the morning does not require any further investigation. This situation is unlikely to satisfy a Venetian. Has our little baby been scared by a creepy crawly in the room or a cold draft in the house? A request goes out to check all the potential sources with a kick from under the covers towards the Martian. This is a timely reminder of who exactly wears the trousers as the house chief during such a parenthood period.

"There is a draught. It is bothering our baby." She may also add, "Don't you care?"

Every door, window, and externally vented appliance would have to be meticulously checked just in case this was the cause of the discomfort. Not only at such an unearthly hour, but the trapping round has to be in the dark with a lighted match. Not just to give sufficient illumination but as a real-time guide as to the severity of any draft. If the flame flickered and bent to one side more than ten degrees, this could be sufficient to warrant further investigation and resolution there and now.

The reaction could have been less than complimentary by the father sent on the mission for a potential draft that hitherto had not been noticed for years and was unlikely to be the reason for the baby's murmur. A howling gale, maybe. But a draught with the strength of a fart? No way. Conclusion? It was his first thought. A non-serious attention whimper.

Let's now consider the too-hot or too-cold scenario for the infant. The supposition is a fairly reoccurring battleground in any household. The 'tog factor' checklist for putting a baby to bed was primarily about the home ambient temperature. Even before the baby arrived, men and women would be at loggerheads over what should be the comfort and warmth of the house. If the thermostat is in a convenient location, such as a hallway, each person is able to sweep past where the temptation of a thermostat re-adjustment is too great. Upwards by the Venetian or down by the Martian. During the energy crisis, the cost of heating fuel doubled. I read a post at Christmas on social media that was a very funny and ironic situation for any UK household. On either side of a heating thermostat controller, which, if turned clockwise, would increase the room temperature, there were two yellow 'post-it' notes. The 'post-it' on the left had written 'LESS PRESENTS'. On the right, if one turned the dial to a lower temperature, the 'post-it' had spelled 'MORE PRESENTS'. I suppose when dealing with babies, these notes could be swapped to be either "more or less children!"

The temperature of the special one is not an exclusive debate limited to being within the home. One should be prepared for a similar exchange when the baby is moved from house to car, from car to various shopping centres or visiting relatives, and back again. The most common expression from the mum to the partner would be, "Is the baby warm enough?" or "Doesn't he/she look hot?"

Such a debate would invariably occur when a Martian had charge of the baby carrier. The normal defence reaction would involve a way of not getting too irritated by the same old-loaded questions. The first line would be the deflection technique. "The baby's body temperature is fine." Martians have learnt that such a response is possibly not sufficient and deemed too lame to halt a questioning glare that spoke volumes, saying, "I don't believe you." The dad quickly refers to his repertoire of minor untruths. Lies would be a little too harsh, but one could say, "I have literally just this minute checked him as you would have done yourself."

Or:

"I have put on/removed a blanket so that he is now comfortable."

Although men may have a tiny tinge of guilt to this approach, it does lead to a more harmonious situation without that bitter feeling in the mouth when your fathering credentials are called in to question once more and just cede to keep the peace.

Cleanliness is next to godliness is the saying many Martians believe is the mantra on Venus. From the moment a new born is taken home from the hospital, the regime of ensuring not a germ or foreign material is present within a cordon around the baby can become a similarly exacting procedure as one could imagine safeguarding a nuclear power station. Sympathy could also be very real for any visitor to the new baby home.

The first words said to visitors arriving at an alpha mum's doorstep would be:

"Hello, nice to see you. As we operate a no-flowers policy, please leave them outside (in common with other maternity units), as we don't want to increase the risk of germs spreading to our baby or, as yet, do not know if they have a pollen allergy. Please remove your shoes and, as advised when you asked to visit us, put on your house slippers. The anti-bacterial soap is in the bathroom, or if you prefer, another station has been set up in the kitchen. Once you have scrubbed your hands for at least twenty seconds and discarded the paper towel into the specific bin disposal facility (as this would be for incineration later), you can proceed into the front of the house. Please do not stroke the dog until after you have handled the baby."

Martians would not mind so much if the newly adopted house rules were only directed at the younger cohort, but the procedure was equally applicable to include all adults and health professionals as well. Any infirm elderly person that required assistance by an arm would, of course, command yet another visit to a sanitiser station.

For men, this is fussiness beyond being reasonable. Our approach was somewhat circumspect and, for the most part, not based on real facts. The belief being that some degree of bad germs is indeed healthy! A too-sterile environment would ultimately lead to less protection for the baby when a situation out of the bubble was unavoidable and certainly later in life.

Like having to play football on pitches festooned with dog turds.

The clever Martian, however, would just crumble under the weight of being visible in relinquishing any resistance to the requirement as laid down by the Venetian. Except that when your closest friends and relatives visit, you greet them first with a low murmur of advice: "You know what she is like. Please just humour her; it would make my life easier."

In such a household, one could see the funny side of any poor pet, which has now been labelled the prime candidate for bringing unsolicited germs into the arena. To see a dog or cat searching for a stroke or the fear etched on the visitors' faces as to whether anybody was prepared to risk the furore of an alpha Venetian by giving the animal a crafty pat. As the particular pets wander through the room, all hands are raised with palms out like a robbery at a bank, ensuring that not a hair of the fur coat would come into contact with the scrubbed-up digits. Moreover, the whimper of a dog with its favourite toy held tightly between the teeth as no grown-up or child is brave enough to pull out from the vice-like grip of the jaw, which by now is drooling with saliva,.

Of course, the extent of this example as to the attempt to keep the visiting room sterile is all well and good, but no one could ever legislate for a dog creeping in where the little tot was lying only to give them a good old slapping lick all over their face.

Let us consider a pretty grotesque area where there could be a significant germ fest or, at best, a less than satisfactory clean environment for the special one. A baby-changing station in a department store or public toilet. Their location can be in a multi-sex toilet facility or, even worse, in some weird design solely in the men's section.

Just for one minute, examine the bandied-around statistic that four out of five men never wash their hands after a trip to the urinal. The reason being that men are not less hygienic, but there are two factors at play here. Firstly, if it is a matter of just unzipping the flies and yanking out your John Thomas by tugging the side of your pants, come on, what has been touched? Barely anything. The second is that once you have loaded your hands with soap, you spend the best part of five minutes trying to wash them off. The 'hot' hand driers 'puff' of warmth through the jet orifices are scarcely powerful enough to make the palms of the hands any less wet than the starting point of having just put them under a tap. Years of adding up all those wasted minutes rubbing hands in front of those infernal machines play on a man's mind, which generally leads to the conclusion that, having not touched anything significant, the whole process is unnecessary.

Nevertheless, he knows there will be a grilling when dealing with the welfare of the baby and has this fact in mind when pulling down the plastic shelf stored against the cubicle wall for the nappy changing procedure. Touched by many human hands and sure, by some that do have a disregard for personal hygiene, it remains a toe-curling experience. To lay your loved one where there are distinct trails of brown staining from god knows what with pretty unidentifiable detritus in the folds of the table can be very nauseating. A further germ hot spot when surveying the room from the corner of your eye is invariably the overflowing nappy bin in the corner, rammed to the hilt with other cherubs' disposables, to which you are just about to add a further layer.

Having tried the upmost to cover the stained changing area with paper towels or any cloth in the changing bag (that does not include the feed muslin) when laying the baby to whip off and on with a clean nappy, it is the smart man who does not mention the state of affairs in the toilet. Reducing eye contact with your Venetian one pushes through the baby-changing entrance door that may still illicit an unwanted response in a manner not anticipated: "I assume it was all clean in there (with no denial or confirmation forthcoming from the Martian), but did I see you touch the toilet door handle as you came out of the room?"

Such a response from a Venetian can be viewed as a red rag to a bull but does create an opportunity for the smartest of Martians to bring to the fore a distraction of the truth technique: "Yes, I did grab the unlocking door mechanism to exit. What else am I supposed to do—fly through it or open the door with my nose?"

Not the normal restrained response for once, but one that gets over divulging the actual shitfest in the cubicle. This would not halt a Venetian from having the last word or some more choice and unwanted advice.

"Don't be ridiculous. All you have to do is drag your jumper over your hand and pull the handle. You have no idea who's been touching the lever."

Sterilisation and sterilising various utensils, equipment, and food for babies brings out yet another different approach adopted on each planet. A Martian's view is a quick swish will do, harking back to the accepted premise that some bad germs are better than an obliteration of all things' microbes. From a dad's perspective, the vigour as approached by mum is in a different league! Using chemicals in the form of tablets leaves a pungent aftertaste. Quite frankly, babies who turn up their bottom lip with such a sterilised teat would be of no surprise. The old method of boiling hot water for a period can be time-consuming and less of a preferred method since the energy crisis of 2022. Who could afford the constant use of this electricity? A funny picture post came to mind. It had two old down-and-outs sitting on a park bench. One said to the other in a speech balloon:

"How did you get here, mate...Did you have a drug problem, get divorced, lost your job, or suffer from PTSD?"

He responded by saying, "No, mate. I just left the immersion heater on!"

We then have the microwave method. The bottles have to be stacked within a container with a certain amount of water required for the correct steam period. The instructions indicate the said volume, and this is one rare occasion where a Venetian would read what the exact process is instead of, under any normal circumstance, being thrown away at the same time as the packaging. However, the phrase 'approximately' is missing from the understanding. Martians are fairly confident that after the first time of its use with a measured quantity of water any other time, an estimate through judgement would only be necessary. Thus saving time to partake in an activity not involving childcare. This practice is fine except in her presence or ear shot:

"What are you doing?" She enquired.

"Filling up the steriliser," he replied.

"You can't do that. You haven't measured out the exact amount. I saw you just fill it up from the tap."

Martians are practical. Noting where the level of water needed to be there was no further reason for the faff of measuring out exactly each time and does not lesson the degree of care as is exhibited on Venus.

Baby's dummies are a further example of a 'keep clean' nightmare. Oh, they work very well as far as the intended purpose, but boy, oh boy, is it difficult to keep every molecule of dirt from the teat? Whenever the baby spits or knocks out of the mouth by an uncontrolled hand movement, the dummy will always take the most direct route to the floor. As a piece of toast landing butter side up under the kitchen table, the dummy would continually fall on the dirtiest, grimiest spot in the room.

As a consequence, so as to avoid the furious cleaning of the dummy each and every time, two methods are adopted by Martians. Firstly, the five-second rule. This has now gained credibility over the years on Mars: if a portion of food or an object that needs to remain clean and sterile hits a dirty surface, you have around five seconds to extract it from the offending area. Thus, counting in your head, you have that time to retrieve the dummy, so all remains tickety-boo. However, it continues to be advisable to check for any detritus substances picked up on the journey downward, such as a ball of fluff or animal hair. Apart from this circumstance, the dummy is good to go.

The second method is to take the American right to silence included in the Fifth Amendment, and if the dummy looks sufficiently clean, deny all knowledge Tommy had spat it out. The premise, of course, is that humans are designed in such a way to be tolerant of germs contained in a bit of hair or dirt. Well, that's what men continue to believe!

It is recognised that the trips to the baby research manuals would have been taken to find a resolution to this problem, but it is contestable that any advice would be given without recognising their practical limitations. A hot water dummy rinse is only conceivable when a tap is available, which is rarely within range. A Venetian would say a solution would be to prepare a flask filled with boiling water each time you go out. Can you imagine this at the playground with all the mums and babies watching for the falling dummies? Any Martians observing from afar would immediately assume the flasks were filled with coffee or tea up to the moment when a little pour of very hot water trickles to the ground on its way past the spat-out dummy. With an active dummy-spitting child, a flask of hot water would be emptied pretty quickly. The mum would consider this dilemma and have a reserve plan. A store of dummies. This would enable a rotation of possibly up to five of the implements, but would still be insufficient for most babies who are habitual dummy cougher uppers, in which case Venetians are aligned to begrudgingly accept the merits of 'The Five-Second Rule'. Of course, other than the alpha mums.

One has to consider when mum and dad go out together. For example, in the play area, dad is in charge of monitoring Poppy's progress, stepping gingerly from one play frame experience to another, and mum is watching, verging on stalking from afar. The dummy falls out. Dad has a quick glance to see if mum noticed and what would be the most appropriate choice from the Martian manual of excuses:

"The dummy landed the right way up and did not touch the floor, dear' or 'Haha, look! I caught the dummy on the way down, and it did not fall to the ground. That was lucky."

and…

"I still have spare dummies in the converted carrier, which is a closable soap dish, so no problem." (With full knowledge, there are no spares and feign the taking out of a fresh one.)

The misunderstanding between the genders in this episode is both a perception and a question of trust. The sense from Venetians of a lack of attention to detail by a Martian not accepting the advice handed out by them, as after all, it is they that have studied all the research. It gives the impression that men don't care as much about the welfare of their children. The argument of Martians is that we are capable of making our own judgements without prompting. Our mannerisms can give the impression we never listen, as it is not in our nature to outwardly admit the requirement of mum has some merit. We just do not like to be directly told what to do. Men just prefer to take time out in their own way, assimilate the information presented, and then take action as they see fit. This may well result in achieving a similar goal in their own fashion. It just sometimes does not appear so.

Group adulation is another sphere where there could be a major misunderstanding. Where does this come from, as it is certainly not a concept known on Mars? Indeed, when this does happen, it becomes a rather cringe-worthy affair for a Martian.

So, we have a quorum of Venetians where the newborn is the centre of attention. It starts with one of the doting females commencing with a string of words directed at the child that can never be understood by the baby but are delivered in a fashion in which they ought to.

"Look at him/her, isn't he/she so handsome/beautiful," one would say, quickly followed up by another.

"Oh yes. Absolutely stunning." Then another.

"Argh. Aren't you lovely? Brrrrrrrrr. Booooooo."

As the demonic high-pitched shrills continue to roll off any tongue—well, except for the Martian keeping tight-lipped, bemused by the situation—he cannot comprehend why a baby requires a new language, verging on complete gobbledegook. Yes, there might be a situation where a slight flexion in the delivery of the form would get a facial flicker from the baby, but is it really necessary for the plethora of expressions such as:

"Yoooooooooooooou are soooooooooo clever boob boob de boob."

Or:

"Has my pretty witty boo boo done a poo poo and need their botty wotty wiping?"

Or:

"How are yooooooo. Yessssssss yooooo, my cherry button."

The uncomfortable situation that could occur is exactly that. The Martian is expected to grasp the thrust of the verbal exchange and fully participate. This is way past most Martians' comfort zone. He has two immediate thoughts. I am definitely not going to adopt this baby speak but will endeavour to maintain a simple but effective language still resembling the Kings' English. The next thought is how to deflect the innermost feelings of embarrassment where there is a Venetian expectation that full participation is an unequivocal requirement.

The tried-and-tested Martian default is put into operation. That of seeking a graceful exit from the proceedings:

'Would anyone like a cup of tea?' Failing this, 'Oh, the grass is now dry enough for the lawn mower. Please excuse me!'

Most Martians have not learnt the concept that if one wants to convince Venetians of credible retirement actions from such a situation, it is no good to show in bold print etched on your face that you really do not want to be there. The misunderstanding can be interpreted by the Venetian huddle as indicating that you have little empathy. The fact of the matter is that men do have a similar admiration for the cherub but would rather express their emotions in a more constrained manner, without an audience, and leave the abject pride to a one-to-one situation with their son or daughter.

The way in which both genders interpret each other's maternal instincts is very much aligned with individual planetary characteristics. Women are more inclined to let their feelings flow with no constraint as the dauphin or dauphine continues to develop. Men from Mars simply don't.

A representative situation, as previously noted, is the photography of the baby experience. For the actual birth, the number of photos needed to be taken would be one every minute (one every second is now possible with many smartphones) to satisfy the mums' insatiable appetite to capture every moment. For the male, the odd picture here and there of quality would be more than sufficient in a non-digital format for any flag waving to their peers. For them, the memory of what has been stored in their subconscious and relived at times when they are in their proverbial man cave gives them the same measure of pride as a mum. In a contrary fashion, a tried and tested Venetian method to recall a detailed step-by-step guide of the days and moments is the infamous

'Baby Book'. If babies were born only to Martians, there would be no such annual, but to the alpha Venetian, it's the life heirloom that cannot be foregone.

As the weeks pass, immunisations that have been administered have some relevance in keeping an accurate record, but to a Martian, other details are just boiler plating. Having had the unfortunate experience of delving into an alpha mum's birth book, there was an extraordinary level of detail that was mind-boggling. It included a full transcript as to what painkillers were taken during the birth, a lock of hair on a weekly basis, what phonic sounds were being made (particularly if they may have resembled 'mum'), and a foot and hand print. Women and men adopt a different sense of need for the depth of a full-plotted history relating to their special ones. A Martian, however, would not dare reproach any Mum who decides such an extreme level of characteristics that chronology would be necessary, but possibly would look to the sky if it went as far as including a swab of vernix from the birth adhered to the book with sticky tape.

In general, it is the male perspective to limit any information for his internal record to a practical level of detail, which he is happy to share. The birth day absolutely. The time and weight at birth, possibly. It may have some useful interest when checking that the growth of the child is consistent with the expectation as a technical exercise, but that would be the extent of what they would share. Not many men would be standing around at the bar of a pub on the birth of their son or daughter, advising their fellow Martians how much they weighed or any other occurrence during the birth just before the traditional wetting of the baby's head drinking session commenced.

There is an undertone of skill level that is a recurring theme between the genders. However, there is one ability the Venetians are far, far superior at. That of multi-tasking. Whatever is needed, women can be more than duplicitous. Men would recognise that females can hold a conversation as well as knitting, cooking, or any other domestic act. Apply this to raising a baby, and they excel in all manner of ways. Breastfeeding is no bar to making a cup of tea or filling up the washing machine for the third wash cycle of the day at the same time. A nappy can be changed with one hand while continuing to keep an eye on any other misbehaving offspring in the vicinity. Martians do not have this skill. They have tried but only execute multi-tasking on a very basic and physical/technical level…when it suits! They need to complete one task before moving on to another. This should be accepted and understood by the mum to resist the temptation to destructively criticise the male in the relationship, creating such examples as these:

"Can't you change the nappy and answer me as to whether you want a cup of tea?"

"Why is Tommy's brother running butt naked in the garden? You should have been watching him."

"Why has Kate buried herself in your dirty underpants sitting at the bottom of the basket whilst putting the other dirty washing in the machine?"

Men simply just have difficulty focusing on two practical tasks simultaneously. In the examples he could not keep an eye on the tot as he fed the bundle of clothes into the drum at the same time or the boy in check at the same time as being preoccupied with changing a nappy.

The final thoughts here are a reversal of perception where indeed there could be a chapter on "Why *can't mums understand blase fathers,"* but this would ruin the mystic of dad's behaviours and potentially be a forerunner for a gender battle not wished on for any discerning reader.

It is not the intention to give too much insight into where Venetian rules are deviated from by Martians, for which the expected behaviour is completely understood, but when out of earshot from the mums, some latitude is taken as to how we men approach bringing up babies if left to our own devices.

Let's start with the pram game. We all know the importance of fresh air. Indeed, when I was a few months old, I apparently spent the whole time in the perambulator (in the olden days!) in the small garden area on my back with only a passing tweeting bird to keep me company. Never, I hear you say. Absolutely true, having this on good authority from my mother! It was part of the advice midwives gave out during the 1950–60s. That of herding all babies outside to take in the fresh air (well, how fresh the air actually was before the Clean Air Act of 1956 or the nuclear isotope strontium 90 in the atmosphere in the spring of 1957!) Except in my mother's case, forgetting to mention this was not meant to involve keeping me outside all day!

For some unknown reason, as part of our Martian nurture programme, men find themselves very conscious when pushing a pram going solo. They attempt first to place some macho zest into strolling along, particularly when a fellow Martian is in close proximity. For Venetians, walking around with a pram has one primary function. To get the little one to sleep. For men, it is about beating the stigma of pram pushing in public by adding some form of bravado fun for the cherub. We like to formulate games and ones that obtain a giggle or smile from the baby even better. To do this, we give the pram a little harder push but at the same time let go of our grip so there is a glaring separation between child and father while orchestrating a 'Weeeeeee' as the action is executed.

At first, the gap is less than a metre but as confidence grows in this motion study, the pushes get harder, counting how many seconds are left before grabbing the handle. A bit like mums counting the length of time when washing fruit. One, two, and three, then grab. This is all fine and dandy until there is either a slight downward hill or bend in the path where the push was far too hard for the track conditions, whereupon abject fear creeps in as you only just recover your position before it is too late. Kate in the pram is by now laughing her little head off, so in this respect the objective was achieved, but with the fear of God now instilled as to how you would have explained away the graze on the head or a trip down to A&E after a catastrophic mistimed lunge resulting in a topple over situation!

Martians will always try and normalise their practical routine in any time-saving or 'hands-free' way when given a task or have the aspiration to continue with whatever they were up to when called upon to be responsible for the care of the baby. This is the only time when a Martian does believe he can multi-task as a Venetian, but in reality, they are simply not in the same league.

Using the TV remote control is difficult with just one hand. Shoving one end into the armpit of the baby can be effective in providing sufficient leverage to get the channels to change and the volume sliders to adjust the sound. No harm done. It's more difficult to continue with baby care when cutting the grass. Stretching yourself between and dragging a pram and the lawn mower is mightily difficult. This technique is nearly impossible if it is a self-propelled type. Try it!

The most versatile and much-called-upon skill is supporting the feed bottle with your chin while still in the baby's mouth as they suck away. This technique is fantastic when called upon, as you can reach for a can of beer that requires opening during that night when mum is out on the town.

Perhaps a chapter would have been fitting to lay bare a compendium of Martian baby multi-function care techniques when mum is nowhere to be seen, but then again...

Chapter 11
Feeding Baby

Excuse the pun, but how we make a meal out of feeding a baby, which is arguably the most natural phenomenon of animals (next, of course, to procreating the species), is beyond the pale for many Martians.

Birds regurgitating their food to feed their young is something we do not have to do. For humans, it is far easier. For the first few months, babies can get all they need by latching onto the mum's breast for their serving of enriched milk to sustain life. Venetians may wonder if there was a design fault on Mars as there was no blueprint for milk ducts in men. Possibly, it was always in the stars (putting to one side the Adam & Eve Bible version) that at the point both planetary beings simultaneously decided to live on planet Earth, each had their own prescribed role. A woman's physiology was crafted to provide very direct nurturing duties. That gave the second being, the male, a further few months during the suckling period to hone their hunter-gathering skills to feed the family.

Moving the clock forward to the twenty-first century, going out into the wilds with a spear and woven basket is no longer a primary requirement. Nowadays, it is simply to seek and find a suitable supermarket with all the produce one could ever dream of and only being laden with a credit card in one hand and a recyclable plastic carrier bag in the other.

A relatively recent adjunct from primaeval to modern days was the introduction of bottle-feeding for milk. In some instances, the 'say no to the breast' was for a legitimate medical reason. More often than not, it was a choice by Venetians, and in the eyes of dads, labelling the reason to give up breastfeeding so as to give an opportunity 'to bond' with the baby is pretty lame. More so he can share in the delights of the night feeds. Thus, with the sharing role comes the customary deviation between the sexes as to how this should be carried out and what constitutes best practice.

For example, Martians have an apparent lack of acute sensory smell for stale milk. If there is a squirt aiming low, missing the mouth, and achieving a direct hit on any clothing, it does not register that this article should now be removed and washed. Venetians, however, have dispatched the offending item into the now mountainous washing pile in seconds. The 'official' clothes basket can no longer be seen but is just a nest of attire in the said corner of the floor. Men would rather limit the faff of washing for as long as possible if they also share in the task of loading the machine. The poor sense of smell is, of course, very convenient to keep the baby dressed far longer in only 'slightly' soiled clothes. It is not to save the odd quid on the water or the cost of the electric bill, as the mums would assume, but it is entirely down to not having to go through the whole washing experience as frequently.

The solution, as advocated by some Venetians once a joint feeding regime has been adopted, is the introduction of a muslin cloth. It is unclear as to how this would fare better than a bib, as it doesn't come with specific ties that could actually be positioned around the baby's neck but have nonetheless become part of the feeding essential equipment. Martians, of course, try to comply, but they just do not seem to have that dextrous ability to position correctly around the cherub to stop major feeding mess incidents. Instead, if an offending spillage or even a spurt of projectile sickness that took no prisoners was to occur, a Martian would forgo the muslin and go for an after-event technique. A paper kitchen towel to mop up first, and then a large tablespoon to scoop up the residue crustation that could possibly now resemble yoghurt or cottage cheese. The final stage of reparation in the Mars book of feeding techniques would again return to the smell test. This is to check whether, even now, there could be a further few days of wear before hitting the washer.

Winding the baby after the feed is viewed entirely differently between the sexes. To men, it is a practical requirement to ensure the baby is comfortable. It is not perceived as a further opportunity to bond as would likely be the emotional presumption of a Venetian. As the requirement to wind is a regular exercise, men are more likely to drift into completely unrelated thoughts such as using this as an opportunity to imagine playing a musical instrument. He contemplates whether an audience could guess that tune as the hand rhythmically taps out on the child's back *baa baa black sheep have you any wool*. After a few times in this role, why not develop the tune so that the additional note caused by a 'belch' could be accommodated as and when it arrives? A favourite would be:

"One man went to mow went to mow a meadow…burp. One man and his dog 'burp' went to mow a meadow."

Martians like to think they can be trusted with most things technical. Through normal life exchanges, they are constantly consulted as to when the possibility of cold weather is to set in and for how long. Is there enough anti-freeze in the car? Is the house water system attaining a comfortable temperature? But wow, when it comes to having the responsibility to gauge the correct milk temperature, that's a completely different matter.

Although even a child would have the aptitude to work out that a few-week-old baby could not drink a substance hotter than what is palatable to them, the dad's effort to warm the baby's milk never quite seems sufficiently skilled as not to require a second opinion. If mums are that distrusting, a Martian solution is quite simple. We do not have to get involved, and the expression 'Do it your bloody self' springs to mind.

As with most of these domestic situations, whether the dads can test the milk warmth to a degree of accuracy that complies with the adopted household standard only generally becomes an issue when the Venetian just happens to be hovering in the vicinity. Such a concern mysteriously disappears when it is a girl's night out; the particular mum wishes for that long and sustained soak in the bath or a trip down to the gym.

There are, however, two methods of achieving the correct milk or food temperature. The Venetians seem to have the notion that the more complex the method, the better the nourishment will taste. There is a suite of heat measuring devices lined up on the kitchen worktop as if heart surgery were to be carried out. A thermometer for any liquid, a probe to get a sense of what's going on within the food, and heat-sensitive bowls to ensure longevity once the optimum warmth has been achieved. For Martians, it's simply a tongue test. For milk, splash and lick on the forearm. For food, a direct plunge of the tongue into the pureed mixture. Venetians can translate this more casual approach as being marginally disinterested in the upbringing of a baby. This is not so. Again, dads are just content to complete a task with the utmost efficiency without overthinking that their baby is so special; nothing short of a meticulous approach would be acceptable.

The internet can be a wonderful tool, but too much of a good thing can raise eyebrows between the sexes as a sense of reality can be lost. Men work on the premise that if one buys fruit, it has already been cleaned and does not need a further wash. From the in-depth research obtained from a website grazing session, it transpires from one of the plethora of baby well-being posts that fruit should be washed for thirty seconds before being introduced into the cherub's mouth. Not twenty or forty, but thirty. It is bleeding guidance, as a Martian would say, and does not have to be taken literally.

This is not to assume the man does not try and stick to the 'house rules' of cleaning fruit with a splash of water. Sometimes it is fairly obvious where there is a spot of field earth left on the offending article and may command more than a quick turn under the tap. It is also true to say that certain vegetables have more dirt cling-on than others. Try getting the peat off a celery stalk quickly! To a Venetian, it still means that the full thirty seconds under a torrent of water has to be applied. I have witnessed such a countdown. Not with a portable counter, a wrist-function stop watch, or a phone app, but voicing out the seconds.

"One and Two and three andddddddddddddddd thirty."

I tip my hat off to that particular Venetian. To be able to sustain rolling the fruit in a cold winter's tap flow, which turned the hands blue for that time with no flinching, but in the comfort that advice has been followed to the letter, is admirable. What's more, this procedure is also advocated for citrus fruit, of which, without exception, the skin is water-tight and gets ripped off to consume the segments in any event.

Unfortunately, this situation has to be marked down as another potential explosive domestic if Dad just happens to pick up the fruit to be washed without thinking that mum is in the vicinity.

"I have been watching you stand by the kitchen door, and those grapes have not had the full 30 seconds under the tap…you are not preparing the fruit properly for Layla."

The Martian has a choice of responses:

"Okay, dearest. I thought I had left the grapes for the full thirty seconds but must have miscounted."

Or:

"They already get washed before they put the grapes in the punnet, so me just finishing them off is absolutely fine. Any longer is a waste of time, delaying more exciting pursuits like watching that snail walk along the windowsill."

The selection will, of course, be down to recognising that our planetary rules are different. Do we want to fight or cede for the greater good? A simultaneous thought that occurs to Martians is how such cleanliness rules are somewhat selective. The thing is, having your balls chewed when not washing fruit correctly is one matter, but apparently, when the special one is whimpering for any number of reasons, it is completely okay to give the child grandad's orange spectacle case to suck, which has been scraped along and put down on all manner of dirty surfaces apart from the crack in his backside.

Chapter 12
Who Had the Hardest Day?

The 'who had the hardest day' topic between the genders is arguably one of the greatest interplanetary battlegrounds when considered at the time life has changed with a new dimension of the family. Sleep deprivation is a major contributor to why each gender has to prove that their day was the hardest of all.

This tension appears to be more of a modern phenomenon. Not that I was around in the 1930s, but observations of previous twentieth-century generations were of a more fixed routine between the genders. As such, there was no debate as to who had worked the hardest. It was all about the assumption as to the adoption of traditional roles between men and women in any domestic situation. Even though we did come to planet Earth from our respective planets, this way of life just continued when a new baby came along.

Take my granddad. He had the same job making musical instruments all his working life. For the full forty-two years of employment, the routine was exactly the same. He would depart at 8:40 am to drive the fifteen minutes from Edgware to Colingdale. The breakfast was always the same: A boiled egg, Weetabix, and a cup of tea poured from a teapot wearing a quaint knitted tea cosy. His lunch hour was timed to the minute; leave work premises at 12 pm; home fifteen minutes later, where his wife would have prepared lunch even with a new baby in hand. As half an hour passed, he would settle down to listen to 'The Archers' radio show, which ran for fifteen minutes. Then a quick peck on the cheek, 'Goodbye, dear', a wave, then back into one of the number of Morris Minor cars he had over the years, back to the factory to complete the hour break. There was never any debate, backchat, or torrent of ill feelings. There was established an unwritten rule not to complain regarding their respective roles and the impact of the degree of tiredness that may or may not have been differential between them. Such a traditional setup was certainly replicated many times over in that era across the developed societies of the day.

It seems now that gender roles are much more undefined, which can invariably lead to what we would now term a Mexican stand-off. Not a singular affair or limited to a particular day, but a recurring debate.

Life between the genders can now take on more of a cynical game plan. That of whom would be revealed as the least tired and therefore, by default, was handed the task of having to get up for the night feeds. A dilemma more poignant to those households where one of the birth partners leaves the home, invariably with a commute to his or her place of work, and the other one is at home looking after the baby. Since the COVID pandemic of 2020–21, there has been more of an acceptance of working from home. More often than not, more time is spent at home during the period of employment. As such, both partners are aware of what is happening in the domestic setting, where periods of inactivity or 'resting' become obvious.

The specific baby's personality or rhythmic pattern can extenuate the 'who had the hardest day' syndrome. A child who is up with the cats at night and curled up sleeping during the day highlights the reasons why each partner wants to end up as the victor.

Those in the know suggest the awareness of a newborn to realise the difference between night and day is about six weeks. The trouble with general patterns is that they never seem to fit your particular one. One of my offspring duly did not conform, and he much preferred to be gloriously awake at night for the next six months.

It was a wrong assumption to view my employment week routine as sufficiently arduous so as to consistently claim victory in the hardest day battle. The commute to work commenced with a forty-five-mile journey along the M4; morning and evening. It later turned into a fifty-mile stretch, but as a glutton for punishment, it was to include the entire circular portion of the M25 from the M1 to Staines. Those parents who have had the displeasure of using a similar journey would sympathise with what needed to be endured. To make any inroads into what would be the time for the drive meant a 5:30 am wake-up call involving a time in the car of ninety minutes arriving in the office before 7:45 am. Having arrived early to the workplace, the 4:00 pm return time was invariably missed due to that last phone call or finishing the final project document. Factor in the twenty minutes needed to hit the motorway system and hey-presto traffic mayhem, giving a minimum journey time of ninety minutes.

Thus, throwing my returning hat into the ring after a twelve-hour day, including at least three hours in the car, gave a solid justification not to be responsible for the early morning feeds or at least a chance to collapse into a comfy chair for at least an hour. My Martian thoughts had already squared whatever the issues of the day were at home; it would not have been as hard as my day.

In analysing how a typical conversation would go, it would kick off immediately at the point of return.

"Hello, darling," swinging an assortment of briefcases and bags laden with files through the door and then flung into a heap at the most convenient spot by the side entrance wall.

The response was the same 'Hi' but with a tone that was the telling description as to how the Venetian day had panned out.

Using the tennis match metaphor once again, the first serve was a short, sharp quip that hopefully would be a scoring point in the 'hardest day' invite-only tournament.

"The M25 sucked today. It was hot (a car model with no air conditioning) and so dehydrated. Can I please just flop in the chair for a moment? (With the intention that this would be far longer and hopefully the offer to obtain a nice cold beer out of the fridge.)"

The second game point was then put forward that five hours of driving had been notched up in the day. Mumm, I noted this was not going to be an easy score as the deafening silence of a pause continued. It dawned on me that I was about to receive a hard and torrid forehand return.

"Whilst you have been gallivanting to work with all that quality time to yourself, in the sunshine, I might add, I haven't stopped all day as **your son** (Venetian emphasis) had decided to be awake all day. What's more, he refused to drink from his bottle, spewing most of the contents back over my shirt. And don't try and interrupt when I start to tell you the mess that pursued when he was trying to eat with a spoon in the high chair."

The game was now in full swing. Before serving again, I tried to remember all that I had learnt from leaving Mars and talking to other Martians as to the skills to deflate such a tricky situation.

I made a good start.

"Oh, my word, darling," I said. "It must have been so tough for you. I wish I was there to help you all day, but we do need my salary, and putting the five hours of commuting aside, I was in a very difficult meeting today that required so much energy. Unfortunately, I need to prepare more notes this evening (well, I could squeeze in time when arriving in the office the next day) before I turn in. I really must insist on getting some sleep tonight." I finished off.

Having really not learnt anything at all, the cardinal sin in this response was committed. Offering a judgement and an overarching reason as to why my day was the hardest in stating 'a salary was required' for the family was, in hindsight, such a glaring mistake. This approach translates into Venetian that the activities I had undertaken during the day were so much more important than any part of her day. The second 'faux pas' was to drop in the word 'insist'. A term which is a red rag to a bull and alien in the Venetian tongue. This made me gracefully withdraw from any further exchanges, leading to the match being abandoned.

It was possibly a case of matchsticks propping up the eyelids for the morning drive and an opportunity to recall all the excuses learnt during the conception phase as to why a late arrival to the office was now likely to occur after being up all night for the feeds.

All was not lost, though, as the hardest-day contest could be construed as a draw. The thought was sufficient wriggle room to assume a 'royal share' for the night duties. It still required good old Martian planning to manipulate the situation, which commenced with our capacity to stay up longer when both parties were tired. A legendary bonus card from our planet. This also gave the opportunity to catch up with a film or a drama deemed unsuitable for joint watching, which sometimes included anything more taxing than a children's programme. The strategy is to stay up and wait to be the last person standing:

"I'm so tired, I cannot get myself up (out of the comfy chair) at the moment," I started. "I still have the notes I need to prepare for tomorrow's meeting. I tell you what, as you are just as tired, you may as well go to bed first. I humbly volunteer for the first feed. You can do the second," I said.

It was invariably the case that my offspring would not require their milk quota until at least one o'clock in the morning. The next feed would likely be the graveyard shift. Anytime between three and six in the morning was the one to try and avoid at all costs.

There however was an obvious flaw in this approach. Venetians are much cleverer and subtle when it comes to manipulating the situation and getting their wishes. The telling sign that would go right over a Martian's head was the cynicism in the response to my suggestion.

"That's so nice of you to volunteer like that. I shall go to bed now for you to join me once our little cherub is fed and made comfortable. I just hope I am not in a deep sleep as it would be so inconsiderate of you to wake me if that was the case. Although I am also so worn out, I am sure that will not be the case," she said.

I hadn't cottoned on instantly to the subliminal message contained within those few words that cometh the hour you are the person that is going to get up. A new lesson learnt was the true meaning of a royal share is one where there is to be no sharing at all should a Martian and Venetian decide to be parents together on planet Earth.

Chapter 13
'Lessons Learnt'

Having read a number of times Dr Gray's book that, metaphorically, men are from Mars and women are from Venus, I unconditionally support his contention that the thought process of the individual genders is so vastly different that it provides the assertion that we must have been derived from two separate planets. It is an observational fascination to consider how each of the planetary dwellers applies their logic at the time they come together on planet Earth to extend the reign of our species. It is with this thought in mind that there has been an attempt to apply such behaviour to an epoch in time. That of when couples decide to embark on creating a family.

The focus has been on heterosexual couples, as this provides the basis for most situations in childbirth. This is not to take anything away from same-sex families. Indeed, as has been alluded to in a number of instances, the plethora of scrutiny where there are so many different reactions would be far less and, quite frankly, would not give rise to sufficient comical material such as contained in this ode to parenting.

The overwhelming thought that arises remains: that of the sum when both genders cohabit gives rise to a greater experience of life. In the converse, if all couples were derived solely from their own planet, life could be dull, dull, dull with no animated situations as there would be a constant consensus in every step of the childbirth journey. We should therefore celebrate the fact that we see the world from two different perspectives.

While the physics of procreation is pretty much set in stone, the journey for any couple is unique, with a number of different circumstances at play. These can also include social, financial, nurturing, or natural impacts. Yes, with respect to nurture, which has been advanced as the most likely formative influence in the male and female definitions, in the past, there was more emphasis on conformity to whatever gender you were. The choice of blue or pink baby clothes depends on the sex of the baby. Football was only for boys, and domestic science was for girls. But will this stereotype dominance continue in the future so that one will be unable to make such a comparison that the genders seemingly do originate from two distinct planets? That question will be left for subsequent generations.

What the examination does bear out is that where the parenting views between genders remain measurably stereotypical, a greater instance of conflict occurs. This is not to say they cannot be aligned, but the nurturing experiences of any individual, male or female, remain very personal.

A constant observation is that no one party has the default to always be right, although from a Martian perspective, he has learnt that in a number of circumstances, it is better to agree with the Venetian for a happy life. Remember, 'happy wife, happy life'. There does, however, remain the need to compromise from the conception stage and through parenthood until the baby attains the stage of interdependency. Being reasonable when the precision method of the Venetians is considered too exacting by the Martians does have merit. Perfection cannot always be realised. The Martian's perception of a more 'that will do' approach is not spawned out of laziness but is a function of their more practical mantra honed through thousands of years judging the level of input that is required for a specific task.

Sometimes those from planet Mars have to ignore the temptation to intercede with their presumed superior logic and take one for the interplanetary couple. It is a skill learnt through life that Martians ought not to add to any hindsight situation with the common phrase 'I told you so'. It is not a lesson learnt by some Martians, which could ultimately lead to a further amount of discourse and unpleasant exchanges.

There have been many examples proffered as couples become parents and are unsure if it ever ends once a commitment is made that you feel responsible for another life. If both sexes understood why each took a different approach and actually said, "That's okay," the stress levels would be far lower. There is no right or wrong approach. Empathy is king and is one characteristic of a Venetian parenting couple that appears more instinctive than with a heterosexual partnership.

Another common difference between the genders highlighted is that Martians just do not like to be organised or told how to do tasks by a Venetian. It may be acceptable behaviour on their planet, but not on Mars. As an adjunct to this would be the undertone of criticism as to which way was best to execute a task or when performance is not to the required Venetian standard.

Misjudgements can also occur as to how each of the parents can stress at the flashpoint. The planetary partner assumes they should react the way they think, which unfortunately starts at the conception stage. It is no good to pass a comment to a Martian enquiring at the point of the prime conception period as to why his 'todger' is not stiff enough. If the problem were in the reverse regarding a Venetians entrance to the tunnel of reproduction, maybe there would be no hesitation in calling for a quorum of their planetary beings to search for a solution. This approach would be abhorrent for your average male. For a Martian, such a reproach at the most critical moment is taken as a condemnation of his manhood, where there is no coming back on this occasion.

A common situation where the mum conducts a sly gaze as dad carries out a baby care task and then offers advice is an unwelcome interjection, which can lead to an immediate lighting-the-touch paper situation of cosmic proportions. If only mums could understand that such a slight as to the way a task is being undertaken is seen as malpractice on Mars.

It is truly hoped that, in some way, analysing the differences in raising babies by gender gives an insight into an important lesson in life. Although men do not have the physical attributes of childbirth, there is still the ability to deliver good parenting. But just in our own inimitable style. Thus, a plea to all the mothers. Please understand us and our parenthetical methods. That, with a little more restraint before exchanging words as to why approaches to the most basic tasks are performed, is not the way a Martian or Venetian would execute, humankind may just—may just—jog along together a little better.